Neille was as determined to get rid of
her unwanted bodyguard as he was to
stay glued to her side. She did her best
to wear him down, to give him the slip,
but Jack Rea seemed capable of over-
coming all obstacles . . .

Books you will enjoy
by ELIZABETH OLDFIELD

DRAGON MAN

What was Ruark Lencioni—her ex-husband—
doing back in Singapore, Katrin wondered.
And now that she had seen him should she—
could she—ignore him? Not that anyone could
ignore the dragon man!

SUNSTROKE

The attraction between Alyssa and Sheikh
Tariq bin Hamed al Zahini was as immediate
as sunstroke, bearing with it all the heat of the
desert. But Alyssa had a job to do, and Tariq
was promised to his young cousin. So whatever
she felt for him could not be allowed to
grow . . .

BODYCHECK

BY

ELIZABETH OLDFIELD

MILLS & BOON LIMITED
15–16 BROOK'S MEWS
LONDON W1A 1DR

*First published in Great Britain 1986
by Mills & Boon Limited*

© Elizabeth Oldfield 1986

*Australian copyright 1986
Philippine copyright 1986
This edition 1986*

ISBN 0 263 75410 3

*Set in Monophoto Times 11 on 11½ pt.
01-0786 – 48507*

*Printed and bound in Great Britain by
Collins, Glasgow*

CHAPTER ONE

'LEWIS'S immediate reaction was to organise personal security.' Mr Trenchard glanced across the dinner table. 'I think that's sensible, don't you?'

Neille paused in licking mango juice from her fingers to grin. 'You mean he's armed himself with a long sharp hatpin? Or has he enrolled for a crash course in karate? Maybe a guard dog would be more his style?' Her grin deepened mischievously as she gouged out another spoonful of ripe golden fruit. 'Maybe not. Lewis would never risk a Dobermann shedding hairs and slobbering all over him.'

'This is a serious matter,' her father demurred. 'The police have been informed and Lewis has requested they launch a full-scale investigation.'

Her grin became a scornful chuckle. 'Isn't that going a bit far? Just because he discovers an obscure little epistle in his in-tray there's no need to——' Neille stopped dead. 'Why didn't he tell me about this yesterday?' she demanded.

'Um.' Suffering a familiar downward plunge of spirits, Mr Trenchard cleared his throat. His daughter's short fuse temper never ceased to alarm him. She could flare up in a moment, and the flash of her blue eyes indicated she might well be ready to flare up now. True, she was restored to her sunny composure with equal speed and never bore a grudge, but in his opinion she was far too headstrong for a young lady, too independent, too self-willed. 'Um,' he prevaricated, 'I suppose Lewis didn't want to spoil your last evening together before he disappeared on his travels.'

'Come clean, Daddy,' she scoffed.

'Um.' Mr Trenchard cleared his throat again. 'Well, he's employed the services of a bodyguard and——'

'A bodyguard!' Neille rocked back with laughter. 'No wonder he kept quiet. I'd never have managed to keep my face straight given that news, and Lewis doesn't exactly appreciate being laughed at.' She giggled, imagining how her amusement would have caused her escort's demeanour to become as bristly as his fair moustache. 'He must be suffering from delusions of grandeur. Who does he think he is—some Getty heir or a pop star?'

'Lewis Mitchell happens to be an important figure in the retail trade,' her father said reproachfully. 'He's managing director of one of the most successful chains in——'

'OK, he's a hot shot,' Neille agreed, intent on stemming the flow. As chief accountant with Mitchells' Department Stores Limited, her father was a company man through and through. For him, the sun rose and set on Mitchells', and never more so than since Lewis had taken control. Mention anything remotely connected with high-street trade, and her father would launch into recitals of past results, present profits, future targets. 'But I still consider he's over-reacting,' she insisted. 'Fancy taking on a bodyguard, that's hilarious!'

'Two bodyguards actually.' Mr Trenchard

gulped in air and continued at a rush, 'One for him and one for you. Your man, a Mr Rea, will be joining us in . . .' he shot a glance at his wristwatch, '. . . five minutes. Lewis tried to fix him up yesterday, but that was too short notice so we had no option but to take the chance of nothing happening in the interim. Thankfully——'

Open-mouthed, she stared at him. 'I beg your pardon?'

'The note did make a threat against "you and yours",' her father reminded her, desperate to utilise this moment of stunned calm to the best possible advantage. 'And as Lewis doesn't possess any close family, the "yours" could well apply to you. Until the police have whoever's responsible behind bars, it seems wise for you to be—looked after. Lewis is picking up the tab and I'm very grateful. These security men don't come cheap. I understand Jack Rea is one of the best in the business. Lewis said he'd been highly recommended. In his time he's guarded ministers of state, visiting dignitaries. There's even a rumour that he once foiled——'

The cornflower-blue eyes sparked. 'He's not guarding *me*!'

'Now Neille, be reasonable,' Mr Trenchard implored, wiping a hand across his balding scalp. His spirits had plunged again. He had known this volatile only child of his would not take the news calmly, known he wouldn't be able to cope. He had never felt properly in charge since she was knee-high. If only Annette had lived, he thought wistfully, surely their daughter would have been far more placid, far more genteel? And surely, given a mother's guidance, she would never have chosen to wear such outrageous clothes? He eyed the outsized sherbet-pink T-shirt which persisted in drooping off one tanned shoulder. High fashion, she called it. But that shoulder was too vibrantly naked to be acceptable at a gentleman's dinner table in mid-October. Her tulip-printed trousers dismayed him, too: they appeared to have been scissored at random from a pair of bedroom curtains. Maybe they had. Neille's multifarious talents never ceased to amaze him. 'Lewis thought——' he began, envying his young employer, now safely installed on the far side of the Atlantic and accompanied by his own bodyguard. 'Lewis thought——' Mr Trenchard wished there was someone around to protect *him*. Where tongue lashing was concerned, his daughter could be lethal. 'He thought——'

'I don't give a toss what Lewis thought. How dare he attempt to hobble me to some hulk!' A spoon clattered to a plate. 'And how dare you take his side? Daddy, you're a traitor. You don't expect me to agree to be trailed around by a—a cross between a Russian weightlifter and a gorilla, without so much as a do-you-mind? That note is a load of baloney. What d'you bet Lewis has been lording it over his minions, as he's prone to do, and someone's decided to strike back? He can be incredibly insensitive at times. He's so busy stamping his personality on Mitchells' that he forgets he's stamping on people, too.' Neille yanked at her T-shirt, exposing even more tanned shoulder. 'Of course, you do realise this could just be an excuse to spy on me? There's an element of calculation in all Lewis does, so it's possible he's making a final check to confirm I'm one hundred per cent squeaky-clean and suitable for the lofty position of——'

'You're being unfair. All that concerns Lewis is your safety,' her father soothed. 'And Jack Rea is nothing like a gorilla.'

'You've met this—this yob?' she spluttered.

'Well, yes.' Mr Trenchard felt his cheeks flush. To grow pink with embarrassment was a pathetic trait in a man of fifty-plus, he accepted, yet regrettably a recurring one. Neille rarely flushed. No demure violet she. Not for the first time he found himself wishing he could soak up a portion of her sturdy self-confidence. He'd be grateful for a fifth; even a tenth would do. 'Mr Rea came into the office this afternoon. He—he had to be briefed.'

'About me?' Her father nodded. 'That's a damned nerve!'

'You'll like him.'

'I will *not* like him. And I will *not* have a bodyguard.' Tempestuously she tossed the mane of copper-gold hair from her shoulders, in an action which would have sent photographers all over London lunging for their cameras. 'I can take care of myself, thank you very much!'

'Sweetheart, your life might be in danger.'

'Pull the other one, Daddy. Someone at his office is playing yah-boo with Lewis, that's all. You said yourself the note was vague, probably the work of an amateur. It doesn't demand money or make specific threats, does it?'

'No, but——'

'Then I refuse to be monitored by a barrel-chested thug with a broken nose and cauliflower ears.'

'Do you now?' enquired an alien voice, and Neille shot round in her chair. Beneath the arch which connected the dining area with the living room stood a tall, dark-haired man. 'Jack Rea at your service, ma'am,' he said, dipping his head. 'Nose regrettably unscathed, ears shell-like, chest——'

'How did you get in?' she demanded.

'Through the front door, how else? Someone had neglected to secure the catch. Not a particularly smart omission considering there's a busy street outside, and taking account of present circumstances.' He extended his hand and walked forward. 'Good evening, sir.'

Having admonished Neille—for she had been guilty of forgetting to snap the lock and suspected he had divined as much—the intruder now switched his attention to her father, allowing her time to take stock. The image of a B-movie thicko who communicated by grunts was way off mark. Jack Rea was lean, elegant and composed; the kind of individual who carried his own natural habitat everywhere with him. His grey eyes were pleasant, yet maybe a shade too pale for comfort. He looked—clever. She had no doubt he had already assessed the well-furnished surroundings, her father's anxiety, her rebellion, and stored the information away. Probably slotted it under appropriate headings, too. Suave in a grey city-style suit and pristine white shirt, he was carrying a briefcase. See the man in the street and you'd identify him as the quintessential stockbroker. Kind of a stiff. Clever he might be, but, Neille decided, also deadly dull.

'Couldn't you have rung the doorbell?' she

protested, slicing through the pleasantries which were being exchanged.

'I did.' He grinned conspiratorially at her father who had risen to greet him. 'But such a ding-dong battle was taking place that obviously you didn't hear.'

'We're just about to have coffee. You'll join us,' Mr Trenchard urged, a hand on the intruder's arm. 'Sweetheart,' he said, over his shoulder. 'Mrs Dawson's left the tray in the kitchen. Be a good girl and bring it through, will you?' Without a backward glance her father led the way into the green and gold living room. He was talking happily, welcoming the younger man into his home, making fun of the 'ding-dong' battle. 'My daughter has a low boiling point,' she heard him chuckle.

Left alone, Neille stood and fumed. In league with this Jack Rea, her father would feel the balance of power had shifted in his favour. Two against one, she thought caustically. But wasn't it three against one? Lewis might be wheeling and dealing in the States just now, and destined to progress on a fact-finding mission through Japan, Hong Kong and Australia, but he had initiated this fiasco. Trust Lewis to barge in without asking and take it for granted he was calling the shots. No doubt he fondly imagined he was getting in training for when she was *Mrs* Mitchell. No way. A bodyguard—huh!

She collected the tray which the housekeeper had prepared and stomped through to the living room. Etiquette demanded Mr Rea be allowed a cup of coffee, but he would then be advised, most apologetically, that he must report back to his superiors with the message that his services were not required.

'Sugar?' Neille rasped, playing hostess with maximum haste, minimum decorum. 'Cream?'

The intruder gave an easy smile. 'Neither, thanks.'

'I believe you used to be in the SAS, Jack?' Mr Trenchard enquired, settling himself down in a comfortable velvety armchair.

Jack! Her father had only met the man that afternoon and already they were buddies. Jack Rea obviously knew how to win friends and influence people, but she was made of sterner stuff. It took more than a smile to dazzle her. Seldom an addict of the softly-softly technique, Neille gave him no chance to reply. If he had been in the SAS, fought lions with one hand tied behind his back, and performed every single stunt in every single James Bond film, good luck to him. But what mattered was getting the man out of the house and out of her hair, pronto.

'There's been an unfortunate misunderstanding,' she announced. 'My father is under the impression I need a bodyguard, but I'm afraid he's mistaken. I lead a busy life and the last thing I require is someone dragging around in my wake. You'd get on my nerves and no doubt I would get on yours.' At this she flung a swift glance defying him to comment, but the grey eyes were dutiful. 'Thank you for your time and trouble, but I shall be remaining a free agent. However, in the unlikely event that I do find myself being pursued by a furtive gent in a trilby and trench-coat, I promise to phone you.' Having curtailed his activities to her satisfaction, Neille decided he should now receive one of her wholesome *ingénue* smiles, smiles which were of inestimable value in the modelling world. 'I have no wish to appear impolite, Mr Rea, and I trust there are no hard feelings, but I'd be grateful if you would kindly hop on your bike and——'

'Aren't you forgetting there's been a threatening letter?' he asked, sipping his coffee. 'I don't think it places too great a strain on the intellect to deduce that someone out there could be gunning for you?'

Neille glowered. If she refused to be impressed by him, it was now apparent he was not impressed by her. So what if she had smiled out from a score of magazine covers and was reputed to be a very pretty girl? She had not knocked the socks off Jack Rea.

'No one's gunning,' she asserted, shaking her head so emphatically that the shining coppery hair swirled around her shoulders like turbulent waves.

'How can you be sure?'

'For the simple reason that the note is a hoax. In any case the "yours" isn't me. Anyone with an ounce of sense must realise "yours" refers to the department stores, or——' She screwed up her face. 'Or—or maybe Lewis's home or possessions.'

Jack Rea exchanged a look with her father. 'At the risk of sounding sexist, couldn't you as his fiancée be deemed to be one of his possessions?' he enquired silkily.

'No, I bloody well could not!'

'Language, sweetheart,' Mr Trenchard rebuked from the sidelines.

'And for your information, I'm not Lewis Mitchell's fiancée.'

'No?' The unwanted guest bent to extract a sheaf of press cuttings from his briefcase. 'Yet it says here——'

'Where did you get those?' Neille demanded.

'From a contact on a national newspaper, a reporter friend. To oblige me he went through their files and was able to come up with——'

'He came up with nothing but tittle-tattle,' she pronounced. Jack Rea's reporter friend might have obliged him, but he most certainly had not obliged her. The relevant cutting would be recent, but the majority had to date back two years and more, and she had no desire to come up slap-bang against the past. 'You don't believe everything you read, do you?' she enquired. 'That engagement was dreamed up by a journalist who had spare column inches to fill in a hurry. Lewis and I are—quote, good friends, unquote.' Smug at having got the better of him, Neille was pert. The war might not yet be over, but she had won a battle.

Jack Rea shrugged. 'Perhaps whoever sent your—quote, good friend, unquote—the note isn't aware of that? The private truth could count for nothing.' He glanced at her sideways. 'Where celebrities are concerned, the only truth tends to be the public one.'

'I am *not* a celebrity, far from it,' she informed him, the crystal clarity of each word warning he had touched on a very sore point. 'I'm a model. One of many. The only reason I ever caught the eye of the paparazzi was by association.' She flicked tapered fingers. 'Any froth which gets reported is without my permission. And ninety per cent's make-believe.'

'My daughter isn't a member of the jet set,' Mr

Trenchard inserted loyally. 'She takes her career seriously and works hard and long, much harder and much longer than most people.'

'I have no doubt she does, sir, but that doesn't alter anything. The public invariably believes the image which the media presents and——'

'Aren't we side-tracking?' Neille bit out. 'Even if I was the "yours", which I'm not, there's still no risk. Lewis takes life far too seriously. Anyone else would have recognised the note as rubbish and thrown it into the waste-paper basket, but typically he goes for overkill. My guess is that a young sales assistant or a kid in his office happened to watch an episode of Hill Street Blues, or some such series, and decided they'd copy——'

'I don't think so,' Jack Rea objected.

Disposing of the final dregs of his coffee, Mr Trenchard pushed himself up from his chair. 'Um, if you'll excuse me I have figures to check for quarter end,' he said apologetically. Neille was in what he termed her 'terrier' mood, which meant this argument was destined to grind on for a long time. He could see no need for him to sit in on it. Jack Rea was supremely capable of coping alone. Indeed, the confrontation possessed more than an element of immovable object meeting irresistible force. Mr Trenchard edged towards the door. 'Mrs Dawson's made up the bed in the spare room so it's ready when you are, Jack. First left at the top of the stairs. Good night. Sleep well,' he smiled, and disappeared.

Neille stared at the intruder who had leaned forward to pour himself a second cup of coffee.

'Are you supposed to be staying the night?' she demanded.

He set down the jug. 'There's no supposed about it, sunbeam, I am.'

'Good grief! Does nobody consult me about anything?' She swept to her feet and stood before him, hands pushed into the pockets of her voluminous trousers. 'I'm sorry to disappoint you, Mr Rea, but there's been a change of plan. I'm a big girl now, and I don't need my father, or Lewis, or anybody to make my decisions for me. This is nothing personal, I assure you, but I must insist that you leave—*immediately*.'

He looked up and grinned. 'Sorry, I don't take my orders from you.'

'But you can't—you can't guard me against my will,' she spluttered.

'No?'

His cool was such that Neille yearned to stamp on his polished black shoes, or kick the shins beneath the razor-creased grey trousers, or tip the coffee jug over his glossy dark head. Anything to rattle him.

'I shall phone Lewis and instruct him to call you off,' she said, her delicately sculpted chin becoming a blockbuster.

'You could try,' he agreed. He pushed back his sleeve to inspect a gold watch. 'Though the time change could pose a problem. Right now your good friend's airborne, somewhere between Boston and New York. When he lands he goes straight off to a business meeting. Your best bet is to wait until two a.m. London time. He's due to check into the Waldorf Astoria around then.' Jack gestured towards the tray. 'Perhaps you'd care to join me in another cup of coffee while you're waiting?'

Neille narrowed her eyes and glared. 'No thanks,' she muttered.

She was tempted to turn tail and flounce off to bed, but it was barely nine-thirty and why should she be chased away? She belonged here; *he* was the intruder. She dumped herself down in the chair her father had vacated and picked up a fashion magazine, rapidly thumbing through. For once the clothes displayed failed to interest her. All she could think about was the man who sat opposite. There had to be a law against a stranger marching into your home as though it was a garrison and taking up sentry duty. From beneath her lashes she subjected him to an intense scrutiny. If he wasn't El Bruto with shoulders like planks and fists like hams, he did look tremendously fit. On reaching their mid-thirties—his age at a guess—many men added a roll of fat around their middles, but Jack Rea carried no surplus pounds. Also his skin had that sheen of good health. He must take regular exercise; perhaps he worked out in a gym with weights, or had sparring sessions. If an assassin shot through the door this minute, how would he react, she wondered. Throw a punch in a split-second reflex? Kick up a foot? Or would he leap to shield her body with his own? Were bodyguards trained to be aggressive or defensive? She did not know.

'Do I meet with approval?' he enquired, breaking the silence.

'Oh.' Neille realised she had been staring at him. 'I was looking for bulges.'

A droll brow quirked. 'Whatever turns you on.'

'Under your armpit, I mean. A *gun*!' she gulped. Maybe Jack Rea wasn't quite such a stiff, after all.

'It's against the law to carry firearms,' he told her, grinning. 'And a weapon would spoil the cut of my jacket. Mind you, if it's any comfort, I have been known to tote a discreet baton from time to time.' He stretched out his long legs, relaxing. 'Your idea of bodyguards seems sadly outdated. We——'

'Now look here, Mr Rea——'

'Jack,' he insisted graciously. 'And I'll call you Nellie, if I may? We shall be living in close proximity for a while, so it's easier if——'

'Nellie!' she cried in horror.

'Isn't it?' He lifted his sheaf of papers from the briefcase and scanned the top page. 'That's what it says here.'

'My name is Neille,' she blazed. 'Spelt N-e-i-l-l-e.'

'The typist put the "i" in the wrong place, that's all.'

'All! Nellie sounds like an overweight char-woman of uncertain vintage, with plastic hair rollers and a cigarette dangling from her mouth.'

'You don't smoke?' he enquired, dead-pan.

'No, I don't,' she fizzed. She was certain he had known her name was Neille. How could he not know? He had been briefed by her father. He had read those newspaper cuttings. Of course, he had known. By pretending otherwise he had deliber-ately set out to rile her. He had been demonstrating that he, too, had some weapons in his armoury. Well, such a tactic deserved a counter tactic. 'While we're on the subject of names, isn't Jack rather prosaic?' she asked. 'Shouldn't you be called Champ or Rocky or something similar?'

The rise and fall of his shoulders beneath the

well-cut jacket accepted the put down. 'Like I said,
you have totally the wrong idea about personal
protection operatives if I may use the jargon. I'm
not one to boast but we have ceased to eat peas off
our knives, and grey matter is now standard
equipment. The bulky philistine who cracked his
knuckles in a corner has gone. Minders also keep
an extremely low profile, as you'll discover. Half
the time you won't know I'm there.' He pursed his
lips. 'Earlier I overheard you tell your father how
you had no wish to be monitored, but it isn't like
that. I give you my assurance here and now that
reporting misdemeanours back to Lewis Mitchell
is no part of my remit. I keep guard, that's all. I
don't snoop. You can rely on my discretion.'

Neille's brows pulled together. 'What misdemeanours?'

'Oh, guys on the side. That kind of thing.'

'I don't have guys on the side,' she said
indignantly.

'You don't?' A strand of dark wavy hair had
disengaged itself from the neatly brushed crop,
and now he pushed it from his brow. 'Then why
all the objections to being protected?'

'Because in my judgment the note is sabre-
rattling, if that, so protection is unnecessary. And
why should I agree to something which is not my
choice? I run my life, not Lewis. And I don't
require you as a support system, Mr Rea.'

'You don't have any—secrets?' He looked
dubious.

'None.' She glanced sourly at his briefcase. 'I'm
well aware most of those press cuttings depict me
as some skittish filly who's perpetually kicking up
her hooves, but if you check closer you'll realise

that any cantering—such as it was—came to an end a long time ago.'

'When Simon Gates died?'

Neille lowered her head. 'Yes,' she muttered. She resented a stranger having access to details about her private life, though he knew only as much, and as little, as anyone else who had perused those gossip columns. Or did he? What had her father told him this afternoon? She began to smart. Jack Rea had no right to pry into her background.

'I don't want a bodyguard,' she ground out. 'I don't need a bodyguard, and what's more I refuse to have a bodyguard.'

'Remember the note,' he cautioned.

'I'm taking that with an extremely large pinch of salt.'

He sighed. 'I don't seem to be getting through to you, sunbeam. That note——'

'Is rubbish.'

'I disagree. You are aware of its contents?'

'Not word for word,' Neille admitted, 'but my father told me——'

'Here.' He took a sheet of paper from his briefcase and thrust it forward. 'Rule one in the security game—learn all the facts you can.'

The paper was a photocopy of the original note. Neille saw that the words had been made up of letters cut from a newspaper and pasted on in uneven lines.

This time you have gone too far. Enough is enough.

Trample any more old values underfoot and you and yours will pay the ultimate price.

Goodbye, Mitchell.

'Gobbledygook,' she announced, displaying a lofty disdain. 'Boil it down and what does it mean? Nothing!'

'You can make one or two deductions,' he dissented. 'For instance, I doubt the note was composed by a kid who'd been watching television. Youngsters don't give much thought to old values.'

Neille shrugged. 'So it was written by an adult. So?'

'By an adult who *cares*.'

'About what exactly?'

'The police don't know yet, but they're working on it.'

'I guarantee they never will know,' she pooh-poohed, scanning the photocopy again. 'If this is anything, it's a warning. Trample on any more values and you *will* pay the price—future tense.'

'"This time you have gone too far,"' Jack quoted. 'That doesn't sound like the future. Neither does, "Goodbye, Mitchell".'

'Dramatics,' she rejected. 'A stereotyped and very garbled threat. Whoever composed this was shadow boxing. It's possible Lewis inadvertently stood on someone's toes, and in a fit of pique they decided to cause him some discomfort in return.'

'How would he stand on their toes?'

'Does it matter?' Neille asked impatiently.

'It mattered to whoever wrote the note,' came the swift reply.

'But why should it matter to you?' she demanded. For someone who had walked off the street and into her life less than an hour ago, he was far too curious. 'I understand the police have mounted an inquiry. Why not leave them to ask the questions?'

'Because I need to compile a dossier of my own.' His tone was steadfastly reasonable. 'I liaise with the police but, without a personal awareness of the people involved, the nuances, a possible motive and any other pertinent details which flesh out a situation, how can I decide the area from which danger is most likely to come? I try to climb into the mind of the enemy; doesn't that make sense?' When he saw she was sceptical, he became impatient himself. 'Do you expect me to stand guard knowing damn all? I have far more experience than to do that.'

'But I don't expect you to stand guard!' Neille shot back. 'And there *isn't* any danger.'

Jack gave an exasperated sigh. 'Just tell me how Lewis Mitchell may have stood on toes.'

'Well, he's been making drastic changes in the department stores and in the process gathered more than a few critics.' She spoke with reluctance. The note was flim-flam, concocted by a little person with little peeves, and by being forced to imagine motives she was granting them a degree of substance. 'As you probably know, in his father's time Mitchells' was old-fashioned, prim and proper, but Lewis is keen the stores should appeal to the masses, albeit the middle-class masses. Days after his father's funeral he brought in time and motion experts, architects, shop fitters, consultants of every type, and a streamlining operation began. Over the past eighteen months or so layouts have been updated, departments switched over to self-service, handwritten stock control replaced by an auto-mated system, that kind of thing. In addition, dead wood has been pruned amongst the staff. Obviously the redundancies, allied with the modernisation, have left many people feeling disgruntled. You've heard about the hoo-ha over Mitchells' advertising campaign, for example?'

Jack nodded. 'Cartoon figures were used in television commercials, and the older employees got up a petition because they felt the image too low-brow?'

'That's right. Actually Lewis had second thoughts about the commercials himself. But all this has nothing whatsoever to do with *me*,' Neille insisted, a hand starfished against her chest in emphasis. 'OK, if Lewis feels he needs protection that's his choice, though I can't see how he's in any danger now he's gone abroad. And I suppose a closer eye should be kept on the stores,' she added grudgingly, 'just in case.'

'A closer eye is being kept. I have guards and dogs organised on a twenty-four hour watch at each of the thirty different locations throughout the country.' He grinned. 'That took some doing at such short notice, I can tell you.'

'*You* have guards and dogs?' Neille questioned.

He nodded. 'I run Rea Safeguards, a security company. Our bread and butter work consists of protecting buildings, payrolls in transit, that line.'

'But if you're the company boss, why——?'

'Why have I deigned to step down from my pedestal and attach myself to you?' He rubbed his fingertips together. 'Filthy lucre, sunbeam. I'd retired from personal surveillance, but Lewis Mitchell wanted me and I wanted my firm to get its claws on his security business, so we did a deal. I agreed to patrol you in return for Rea

Safeguards having a crack at patrolling his stores and warehouses. The regular firm has been stood down for a while, and if our performance is sufficiently impressive maybe they'll be stood down on a permanent basis.'

'In other words, I'm the thin end of the wedge? Thanks for the compliment!'

'You should be pleased your boyfriend cares so much about you,' he replied.

'Well, I'm not.' Neille's original resentment returned to the fore. 'He has a cheek, fixing you up behind my back. I suppose he imagines I'll give in gracefully, but no way.' She shot Jack Rea a look which would have downed a stampeding elephant at fifty yards. 'I'm not being hounded.'

'It won't be that bad. I'm house-trained and quite cute once you get to know me.' His grin faded. 'Why not accept we're stuck with each other and co-operate? Then it'll be easier all round. Hell, chances are I'll only be with you for a month at most.'

'A month!'

He nodded. 'A month is what your good friend requested. I've been asked to stick with you all the time he's abroad. Naturally if the police detain whoever's responsible for the note, I'll make an earlier exit. On the other hand, if more threats have surfaced by the time the situation's reviewed in four weeks' time, I guess my duties could be extended.'

'Over my dead body,' Neille scythed.

Jack Rea gave a slow smile. 'Sunbeam, I'm here to make sure it will never come to that.'

CHAPTER TWO

NEXT morning Neille rose early. Washing as quietly as she could, she pulled on denims and a navy mohair sweater, caught up her hair in a fancy clip, and tiptoed downstairs. The house was dark and silent. Cold, too, for the central heating had yet to click on. Her father's alarm clock wasn't due to ring for another fifty-five minutes and there had been no sound from the spare room. As she devoured a bowl of muesli and her regulation half pint of fresh milk in the kitchen, shivering a little, she polished her plans. It would be the middle of the night in New York, so a phone call to Lewis was out, but in any case contact had now been reserved for later. She needed time in which to nullify the opposition. Today the oh-so-clever Mr Rea was destined to be left stranded. The moment her breakfast was finished, she would be out of the house and away. A series of appointments with the hair salon, photographers, model agency, etc., had been pencilled into her diary, so she would be fleeing around the city at breakneck speed. Jack had small chance of finding her. If, by some fluke, he did manage to make contact at one location, all she had to do was outwit him before she landed at the next.

Neille grinned, visualising the phone call at the end of her day when she would scathingly advise Lewis that his bloodhound had a lousy sense of smell. That would make him stop and think. If she followed on by stressing her determination to run her life *her* way, she had no doubt the end result would be—goodbye, Mr Rea. A night's sleep had done nothing to shake her conviction that the threats were not worth the paper on which they were pasted. Only if, and it was a million to one if, a second note materialised, would she revise her views. For now she intended to carry on as normal.

Pushing her arms into her fur jacket, she slung her tote-bag over one shoulder and, avoiding a creaky board in the parquet-floored hall, unlocked the front door. Pale colours of dawn were streaking a wintry sky.

'Cold for October,' Jack declared, appearing beside her like a genie from a lamp. He looked snug in a camel coat. 'Wouldn't even be surprised if we had snow. Are you a jogging freak or is this a variation on the moonlight flit?'

Head down, Neille searched in her bag for her gloves. Damn the man, his appearance was a deliberate obstruction of her liberty. He must be a very light sleeper. Light on his feet, too. She hadn't heard him moving around.

'I have work to do,' she replied saltily.

'So early? I realise modelling can't be the ritzy life it's cracked up to be, but I never knew it comprised night shifts.'

'I like to start my day with a brisk walk.' Where were those gloves? What the hell! She drew her collar around her ears and plunged feverishly off along the street. 'The exercise tones me up,' she said curtly, as he used long fluid strides to keep pace.

'I'd have thought it'd have worn you down,' he replied.

Apart from a milk float and a shambling postman, they were the only people on the move, though the occasional light which shone behind upstairs curtains indicated that the rest of the world was beginning to stir. As she walked, shoulders hunched against the icy wind, Neille realised she could be fairly said to have shot herself in the foot. So engrossed had she been in her aim to put space between herself and Jack Rea, she had neglected to line up a bolt hole. Where did she go now? How could she pass the time? Her first port of call was the hair salon, but that didn't open for another hour and a half. And to think she could have been tucked up warmly in bed!

'The catch needs fixing on that small window in the kitchen,' her companion informed her, his breath making white clouds. 'It's a weak spot. And an additional bolt on the front door wouldn't go amiss.'

She came to an abrupt halt. 'You've been snooping,' she accused.

'I've been doing what I'm paid to do, ensuring your safety.'

'Huh!'

Neille resumed her march. It was far too cold to stand and argue. Her nose was nipped and, one by one, her fingers were losing their feeling. Too late she remembered she had left her gloves on the hall table. She cast a glance sideways. Jack had gloves, robust leather ones. They would probably be fur-lined. Damn his gloves! Damn him! Veering right, she tramped with her escort past a small park, then crossed left and left again, bringing them to the neighbourhood's main shopping area.

Dummies smiled incessant smiles in brightly lit windows and neon signs flashed, but interiors remained dark and doors were stubbornly labelled 'closed'. She was a dummy. Why hadn't she waited until a decent hour before eluding Jack Rea?

Neille searched up and down the street for a taxi, but in vain. She heaved a sigh. She would have to use the Underground. Off she headed, Jack in tow, prepared to slog it all the way down the hill to the tube station, when lights suddenly flickered on in a cafeteria.

'I'm having a hamburger,' she announced, swerving towards it. 'Want one?'

He winced. 'At this hour? No thanks. Coffee'll do me.' They made their way through a maze of red and yellow plastic-topped tables to a counter where a yawning chef in grubby whites was attempting to face the day. 'My treat,' Jack said, when, after a lengthy wait, their order was handed over.

'Thanks,' Neille replied automatically, and marched off to find the cleanest of the tables.

'For what?' he asked, joining her. He gazed around, taking note of the smeary windows, the overflowing ashtrays, the packets of sugar which were long-term residents of a stained saucer. 'You didn't exactly bring us to the Savoy Grill.'

'Don't be picky,' she snapped. So calling in at the cafeteria had been a mistake, but it was his fault they were here in the first place. Must he criticise?

Jack took a mouthful of coffee and grimaced, then made doubtful eyes at her plate. 'Should you eat that? It's swimming in grease. Won't it give you spots?'

'I never get spots!'

He cowered back. 'Don't bite my head off. Not only were you up far too early this morning, you also appear to have got out of the wrong side of bed.'

'OK, I'm not all sweetness and light,' Neille retaliated. 'Would you be if someone had lumbered you with a Siamese twin without so much as a by-your-leave?' His rueful smile managed to calm her down a little, and when she next spoke her tone had become reasonable. 'Maybe Lewis thinks that note is for real, but I don't. What's more, I doubt very much if you do either. Be honest, Jack,' she coaxed, using his name as deliberate encouragement, for she also knew a trick or two about winning friends. 'You've had experience of these things. You don't genuinely believe I'm in any danger, do you?' He frowned, but she ploughed on. 'I accept that by nature of his position as a company chief Lewis can't avoid the odd enemy, known or unknown, and that maybe there's a chance, just a slight chance,' she qualified, 'someone might be conducting a vendetta, but my case is different. I don't rearrange people's lives. The influence I wield is zero. I'm just an innocent girl who——'

'Innocent?' He almost choked on his coffee. 'Are you professing to be Rebecca of Sunnybrook Farm? If so, I'm afraid it won't wash.'

'No, I'm not.' Neille pushed the hamburger around her plate. One bite had confirmed her fears. Not only greasy, the hamburger was as tough as old boots. 'But I can't believe I've inspired such impassioned feelings that I've wound up as somebody's target.'

'The world has more than its fair share of crazies. How can any of us know what a twisted mind will decide?'

'You're only saying that because traipsing after me for a month is good news for Rea Safeguards' balance sheet,' she retorted, forcing herself to keep on eating. She wasn't going to back down, not with him watching.

The disobedient strand of hair had once more tumbled on to his brow, and Jack raked it aside. 'I'm saying that because unfortunately it happens to be true. You read the papers, watch television. You know how people can be gunned down by complete strangers.'

'I know that you've played the terrorism game far too long, zonko! I'm not one of your controversial figures.' Neille rammed in another piece of hamburger. 'I'm *ordinary*.'

'Don't speak with your mouth full. Yes, very ordinary. You're a commonplace model who's featured in glossy magazines on a regular basis. You travel the world on assignments, you can earn more in a day than some people earn in a month. And it's on record that you've driven around in fast sports cars with fast young men——'

'Man!' she flashed.

'Man. And danced naked in fountains.'

Neille's blue eyes burned. 'You're as bad as the newspapers, continually harping back to the past,' she complained. 'And that damned fountain incident was a complete misrepresentation of the truth. You don't know the whys and wherefores. You don't know that I'd been forced to go into the water because Simon had——' She brought herself up short. Why was she explaining anything to Jack

Rea? The past was a closed book and better left that way. There was no need to justify her actions to a bodyguard, to a man she barely knew. All the same, she wouldn't want him to think she was candy-floss. 'The fast cars etc., happened when I was younger and far less mature. Peace of mind and sanity are what matter to me now.'

He pulled down his mouth. 'Very sensible. How old are you—twenty-two going on seventy-five?'

'You've been briefed. You know full well I'm twenty-four,' Neille replied, thrusting aside her plate, clear at last.

The grey eyes rolled to the ceiling. 'So old,' Jack sighed. 'So old.'

Dominic, the hair stylist, had overslept, which meant that in addition to a freezing fifteen minutes spent rubbing her arms and stamping her feet in the doorway—to Jack's ill-concealed amusement—Neille then suffered a long period in the chair while the juniors mopped the floor around her. The image which looked back from the mirror was uninspiring. Her face had become a red and white blotch, with shadows the colour of black grapes beneath her eyes. Make-up would conceal the worst, but one of her greatest assets was a sparkly vitality and right now anyone who had crawled out from a Siberian hedge would have displayed more sparkle. She should never have persevered with that hamburger—it lay like a lead weight in her stomach. If she went down with food poisoning, she would not be surprised.

Much to her irritation, Jack looked none the worse for their cold and premature start to the day. By angling an oblique search through the mirror, she could see him in the jazzy black, white and purple vestibule. He was chatting to the blonde receptionist. The minute the salon door had been opened, he had shed his coat and made himself at home. Not much later he was installed at the reception desk, using the phone to contact his office and various outposts, while the blonde flitted around providing ballpoint pens and paper, and smiles which represented a criminal offence so early in the morning.

Neille was grateful when Dominic arrived and transferred her to the back-wash bowl, where the reflected figure of Mr Rea and the girl dancing attendance could no longer annoy. Involved in the routine of having her hair shampooed, conditioned and rinsed, she began to thaw out.

'I take it that guy's with you?' Dominic enquired, flexing comb and drier with matadorial finesse.

'Yes, he's——' What did she say? Never 'he's my bodyguard', because a statement like that would have the hair stylist downing tools and demanding to be given full details. A bodyguard was a rarity in anyone's world, and Dominic would be fascinated. Gossip was the staple of life for the satin-waistcoated young man, to be distributed among his clients all day and every day. But the last thing Neille wanted was to be gossiped about. Her days of providing hot news were over. Dead and buried, like Simon. She also baulked at describing Jack as a 'friend'. Dominic's translation was bound to be 'lover', and the gossip would still flow, if along a different channel. '—an admirer,' she settled for. 'But he's a pain and I'm trying to avoid him.'

'Looks a dish to me, ducky,' the stylist protested, sneaking a peek into the vestibule. 'The suit might be straightsville, but don't you have a feeling that beneath it he could be all animal?' Dominic gave a delicious shudder.

'He is all animal—rat.' She crooked a finger to draw him closer. 'When I'm ready to leave, could I use the back door?'

'Whatever you fancy. Mine is not to reason why, mine is just to wash and dry,' Dominic chanted, going off into peals of manic laughter.

Neille settled her bill discreetly and slipped out to the cloakroom at the rear. Knotting a silk square over her head to protect the flamboyant curls and twirls from the tug of the cold wind, she put on her jacket and gathered up her bag. The salon was set mid-centre in a terrace of shops which backed on to a parallel terrace. A narrow alley ran between them and as she emerged on to it, Neille grinned. No sign of Jack. So far, so good. His telephone calls had been completed and she hadn't heard his voice or caught sight of him for ages. No doubt he would be drowsing in the vestibule beneath the receptionist's simpering gaze, or had maybe gone round to the snack bar next door for a decent breakfast. Whatever, when she reached the end of the alley and peeped out, the coast was clear. A woman hurried by pushing a baby buggy, three workmen were digging a hole in the road, other people came and went, but there was no tall, dark-haired man in a camel coat.

Chuckling, she waltzed to the kerb with carefree steps. Her next venue was a studio in Chelsea, and for that she required transport. Conveniently a black taxi was approaching, its 'For Hire' flag clearly visible. When the driver stopped in response to her wave, Neille quoted the address and reached out for the door handle. A gloved hand arrived there first.

'Allow me,' said a burnt-toast voice. 'And may I award you seven out of ten for trying?'

Detective Inspector Brian Gilchrist took a swig of beer from his glass, wiping the froth from his mouth with a pudgy fist. 'What is it now, my old mate—three weeks down and one to go?'

'Almost,' Jack agreed. 'Thank God.'

'Still giving you a hard time, is she?'

'Hard! She's had me on my toes since day one. I feel like I've aged ten years in the process.'

Grinning, Brian opened out a Sunday colour supplement magazine and spread it on the bar table. 'She's beautifully packaged,' he said, voice hushed with admiration. Under the heading 'Fashion Goes The Way of All Flesh', Neille frisked, strutted, tantalised in a variety of outfits, most of which featured a bare midriff and lots of leg. 'What can you find so bad about guarding a body like that? I just wish someone'd give us middle-aged coppers half a chance.'

Jack pulled a face. 'Silent, I agree she's a knockout. Verbal?' He shuddered. 'I'd fondly imagined Kay had exhausted the insult supply prior to our divorce, but Nellie thinks up new ones every day.'

'Nellie?'

'In-joke. She hates it, so I call her that whenever she needs cutting down to size. Like every five minutes.'

'Don't tell me the two of you have yet to become *simpatico*?' the policeman queried, plump cheeks splitting into a smile.

'Ha ha. It's been war ever since she realised Mitchell wasn't going to give me the push.' Jack frowned at the photographs. 'I wonder what he thinks about these? He came over as a most fastidious gent.'

'Stiff and starchy,' Brian agreed. 'I expect he turns a blind eye; what else can he do? It's not as if he's married to the girl and can put his foot down. Though I imagine marriage is on his mind? Who wouldn't fancy snuggling up to that gorgeous little creature every night?'

'Yours truly for a start,' came the prompt reply. 'But I can't imagine them as Mr and Mrs. In fact, it amazes me they're even what Neille calls "good friends". Mitchell's not her type. What the hell can she see in the guy?'

'Never heard of power and wealth, those two supreme aphrodisiacs?' The policeman took a mouthful of beer. 'Is Mitchell still returning home as planned?'

Jack nodded. 'Neille and I hop over to Paris next week for a quick visit, the following Sunday I complete my stint, and he flies into Heathrow late Monday afternoon.'

'You're accompanying your young lady to gay Paree, city of love?' asked Brian, ogling the magazine again.

'Yeah, though she's made it agonisingly clear, in her inimitable way, that she'd far rather do the trip solo. She's landed a modelling job for a fashion house over there, photographs taken by some big noise called André.'

'And you're moseying along?' There was a groan of envy. 'Some blokes have all the luck.'

'Don't you believe it. I've managed to keep one step ahead so far, but how I'll cope over there remains to be seen. I've visited most places in Europe, but oddly enough I've never been to France. Which means I'll be dancing in the dark. Also my French is limited to basic requests, like please pass the butter, and a handful of obscenities. What do y'know but I'll be mouthing those obscenities next week?' Jack unfastened his black leather jacket and spread his legs. 'My guarding Neille has developed into a kind of contest, you see. She has this overwhelming desire to lose me. I know it, and she knows I know it.'

'She's not afraid of being picked off by a hidden marksman if she goes it alone?'

'She's not afraid of anything!' he responded, with a dry laugh. 'Funny thing is, when Derek's on duty, like now, she's good as gold. Then I appear and we're back to cat and mouse.'

The policeman chuckled. 'And mousie's hoping to sneak off down a hole when you're in Paris?'

'She'll try, like she tries here. To be honest, Brian, I've had one or two tricky moments already; not that she knows. Fortunately my working knowledge of London and its back streets means that on the odd occasion when she's gone missing I've managed to pick up her trail pretty quickly. Her hair's distinctive, which is a big help. If I look along a crowded street I can pick her out straight away.' Jack laughed, tugging at an ear lobe. 'Mind you, I once went hurtling after this redhead and it was only when I drew level that I realised the woman I was chasing was fifty if a day, and the colour had come courtesy of a bottle. I was very tempted to tell Neille. She'd have been furious.'

'Vain, is she?'

'Funnily enough, no more so than any other woman. She takes care of her figure and her looks, she wouldn't be a successful model if she didn't, but they're no big thing. She doesn't give a damn about me seeing her with a scrubbed face and hair uncombed first thing in the morning.' He gave Brian a look. 'And you can stop that lascivious mind of yours from working overtime. First thing in the morning means when she emerges from her bedroom and I emerge from mine. Any contact between Miss Trenchard and me is strictly business.'

'No nocturnal solace for the damsel in distress?' The policeman's eyes were twinkling behind his glasses. 'Whatever happened to Jack Rea, super stud?'

'He grew up. Now I drop everything when I'm working, women included.'

'That didn't used to be the case. Women more or less *were* your work, once upon a time.'

'No longer. Now all my energy goes into Rea Safeguards. It's been ages since I've had the time, or the inclination, to pay court.'

'You've lost interest in sex? Come off it, Jack.'

'I've lost interest in casual sex and shack-up deals. When I think how I behaved in the past—Well!' He shook his head in disbelief. 'Don't laugh, but my aim now is to build a nest, a permanent nest, and rear some chicks. The problem is, who with?'

'You're not telling me you're fresh out of beautiful women? My God, you'll have me in tears.'

'No.' He wiped a trickle of condensation from his glass and sucked his finger. 'There's a girl at the model agency. A secretary who's been slipping me Neille's timetable on the sly. Dee's a pretty little thing. Friendly, reliable. I might take her out some time.'

'Big of you,' Brian commented.

He laughed. 'Now you're starting to sound like Neille.'

'She slaps you down?'

'With no paltry skill. She gets so damned frustrated at not being able to shake me off that in retaliation she hurls abuse. I've come in for some pretty heavy flak. If my ego survives this month intact it'll be a miracle.'

'Non-stop aggro?'

'No, not non-stop,' Jack admitted. 'Even Neille couldn't manage that. There are lulls when we share a joke, have a decent conversation. On the odd occasions when she forgets how much she objects to my presence, she's actually good company.' He had a drink of beer. 'She even rescued me once. I was waiting outside this ladies' loo when——'

'Kinky!'

'And how,' he agreed. 'But Neille's developed a fetish for disappearing to powder something or other, which means I get to spend a goodly proportion of my time hovering around outside unsavoury places. It appeals to her sense of fun,' he said wryly. 'However, I'd been hanging around there like a spare part for quite a while when one of your uniformed boys appears. He begins to take an interest and, after dispensing a series of suspicious glances, starts off towards me. I quake. I think, "God! I'm about to be arrested for loitering with intent." Your boy is just about to start up with the "'Allo, 'allo, what 'ave we 'ere then?" when Neille appears. She tumbles to the situation in a flash and leaps on me crying how sorry she is to have kept me waiting, what a pet I am to be so patient etc., etc. Thankfully the constable goes into reverse. It's rare she does me a good turn, but I have to confess she did on that occasion.' When his friend's laughter had subsided, Jack frowned. 'Speaking of your boys, I don't suppose anyone has managed to solve the mystery of Mitchell's nasty letter?'

''Fraid not. We've done the usual enquiries, but drawn blanks all round.'

'There's no one who actively hates his guts?'

Brian scratched his chin. 'No, though the guy possesses a real flair for upsetting folk. He's bursting with bright ideas, but consistently puts them into action without bothering to consult those involved. In consequence, they take the huff. Like your young lady.'

'Except that she's turned taking the huff into an art form! But you're right, I don't think it's me personally she resents so much as Mitchell springing me on her. The way he tries to manipulate is what really gets up her nose.'

'Understandable. For "diplomat" you can read "steamroller" where our store boss is concerned. A prime example is how he dealt with the old guard after his father's death. Most of the directors were doddery old duffers who should've been put out to

grass long before, and if Mitchell had employed an
ounce of tact I'm sure they'd have been happy to
go. Instead he goose-steps in one morning and
dishes out dismissal notices. *And* he forgets about
golden handshakes or thanking them for past
services. Eventually it was smoothed over, but
some of the blokes we interviewed went an
unhealthy shade of puce when I mentioned his
name.'

'So you've not moved any further down the
trail?'

'Nope. If we had you'd be the first to know. But
we both had a hunch those threats weren't going
to amount to anything and now, after three weeks,
we've been proved right. You can bet your bottom
dollar that whoever wrote the note isn't about to
despatch another one. He just wanted to get the
bile out of his system.' Brian fixed his glasses more
securely on his nose. 'You've never seen anyone
acting suspiciously in the vicinity of your young
lady?'

'Not a soul.'

'Strange that newspaper photograph of her and
Mitchell should've been pinned to the letter. I just
wish I could work out its significance.'

'Don't we all? It really terrified her father,
though he's managed to calm down a bit now.
Old Trenchard lives on his nerves. It amazes me
how he ever managed to produce a daughter like
his.' Jack took another swig of beer. 'You
realise she's still being kept in the dark about the
photograph?'

Brian nodded. 'Mr Trenchard insisted she
mustn't be distressed.'

'Fat chance.' His lip curled. 'It'd need knives

whistling past her ears before that one'd be distressed.'

'Don't be too hard,' came the appeal. The policeman considered the girl in the colour supplement was a sweetheart, fresh and beguiling. 'If she's a bit of a toughie, perhaps she'd had to be? Who can tell what knocks she's taken?'

'Knocks? She doesn't know the meaning of the word,' Jack derided. 'Believe me, Brian, fairy godmothers were out in force the day Neille Trenchard was born. Not only did they bestow a face and figure which guaranteed a top-notch modelling career, they also provided a father who spoils her rotten, a current boyfriend who's as rich as Croesus, a previous boyfriend who was so damned handsome it makes you want to throw up, a——'

'You mean Simon Gates? That's right,' the policeman grinned when two surprised brows lifted, 'you're not the only one who's done his homework.' His grin widened. 'Actually it was Moira who filled me in. I happened to mention I'd had dealings with Mitchell, and lo and behold my wife knew more about him and your young lady and golden boy Gates than the whole of Scotland Yard put together. A great gal for the gossip columns is Moira.'

'Beats folding doilies all day, I suppose.'

'You male chauvinist, you! And now I'm sounding like your young lady again—right?'

'Right. And my young lady, as you call her, is in for a nasty shock next week. So far I've allowed her a very long length of rope, but the time has come to pull it tight.' Jack's eyes narrowed into a lethal squint. 'One way or another Miss Neille Trenchard will realise she's met her match!'

CHAPTER THREE

FREEZING fog had delayed all flights out of
Heathrow. There had been a wait in the lounge
before the boarding call came, a wait at the gate,
and now on the aircraft little was happening.
Stewardesses wafted back and forth wearing fixed
smiles, at ten-minute intervals the captain gave
apologetic messages of hope, passengers grew
restless. Neille peered out at the thick white
blanket which comprised the view, and sighed.

'Aren't you sorry you insisted on coming to
Paris?' she enquired, turning to her companion
who was examining the safety instructions for
what had to be the third time.

'I didn't insist, Lewis did.'

'Jack!' she remonstrated. 'You know darned
well that if you'd told him there was no danger
he'd have been happy to go along with that.'

'Would he?'

'Yes. He listens to you. Grief, *you're* the
professional.'

He slung her an amused look. 'Do I hear faint
praise?'

'Not a whisper. I'd never praise a man who uses
his reputation to get what he wants, with no
thought for others.'

'Others being you?'

'Who else? More than three weeks have gone by
without me paying the ultimate price of being
chopped up into little pieces and fed to the

crocodiles, so why can't you admit the note was
pure unadulterated——'

'Language, Neille,' he cut in, grinning.

'Beast.' She sat for a moment, then compulsively
tried again, even though last minute efforts were
futile. 'Look, Jack the Ripper isn't going to follow
me to Paris, so why must Jack the Pain-in-the-
Neck?'

Realising the Japanese businessman on his other
side had begun to take an interest, Jack adopted a
woebegone air. 'Oh, sunbeam, you know how
fragile I am emotionally and how you wound
when you say such things. After these three
wonderful weeks, during which we've built up such
a——' He placed a hand over his heart. '——
meaningful relationship, I had hoped you'd have
wanted me close. I don't ask much. Sleeping on a
mat outside your door would be enough to keep
me content.'

'Sorry to ruin your day, but there's a distinct
possibility they don't have mats outside the doors
at the George V,' Neille replied. She tossed the
Japanese gentleman a throwaway smile, but he
continued to listen undaunted.

'That's fine.' Jack stuffed the safety card back
into the seat pocket. 'Because we're not staying at
the George V.'

'I am,' she said, crisp with conviction. 'The
agency arranged the accommodation through the
fashion house. A luxury pad happens to be one of
the perks.'

'Sorry, but Dee——'

'Dee?' Neille spat out the word. 'What's she got
to do with anything? The way that girl drools over
you is sickening. Obviously the poor creature's

short-sighted in addition to being just that teeny-weeny bit cross-eyed. How she ever manages to type straight is a miracle.'

'Dee has altered the accommodation,' Jack said heavily. 'At my request.'

'She hasn't?' Neille saw his face. 'She has! My God, you really are a——'

'Beast?'

'Pachyderm,' she slammed.

A frown from the Japanese interloper indicated his English had let him down.

'A very large thick-skinned mammal,' Jack translated, and received a grateful smile.

'You think I'm not smart enough to realise this cancellation of the George V represents yet another of your attempts at one-upmanship?' Neille demanded.

'There you go again, accusing me of base behaviour,' Jack parried with a grin. 'All the cancellation represents is safety procedure; you must have heard of it. Keeping our heads down makes sense. We're staying in a discreet little hotel in the fifth *arrondissement*. It might not be as fashionable as the George V, but Dee assures me it's clean and comfortable.'

'Dee would.' She ripped the zip of her snowy white parka higher towards her throat, as if protecting herself from pollution.

'Sunbeam, why not resign yourself to the fact that I'm with you until next Sunday?' he appealed. 'That's six days, a meagre six days, that's all.' He leaned closer, turning his back on their Japanese audience. The man had seen enough, heard enough. If he wanted to inspect a pachyderm's shoulder blades at close quarters, that was up to him. 'Can't these last few days together be a time of peaceful co-existence? Why not allow *entente cordiale* a chance?'

'What, give up just when I'm warming up?'

'Why not?'

Privately Neille had to admit the idea was tempting. In three weeks of determined effort she had never managed to elude him—not properly—and it seemed doubtful she ever would. But a principle was at stake here. She refused to go soft and bow to his superiority. If she gave up now Jack would win and she would lose, by default. No, she was determined to keep on fighting to assert her independence right until the bitter end.

'What's the matter?' she taunted, giving him an arch look. 'Frightened I might wriggle out of the net once we arrive in Paris?' She glanced at the foggy outdoors. '*If* we arrive in Paris.'

'I'm not frightened of anything,' he vowed. 'I've kept tabs on you in London and I can keep tabs anywhere. I have a highly successful track record; why should Paris be any different?'

'But it is.' Neille raised a slender finger and drew it lightly down the front of his jacket. 'Look at you. We're not even off the ground and already you're different. Gone is the middle-of-the-road stockbroker and here is the—what, macho tourist? Chunky sweater, leather jacket, jeans and sneakers. Myopic Dee would consider you're very . . . sexy.' She pronounced the word as though the letters were eggs, splattering from a great height.

'Leave Dee out of this,' he barked, and she realised he was annoyed.

Strange, for if their time together had taught her anything, it had taught her that Jack Rea possessed vast reserves of good humour and control. How he had maintained his calm in the face of her provocation, she did not know. Neille would have socked herself one ages ago. Yet he suppressed any urge to hit back. He had *had* the urge—often. His grey eyes would narrow, his jaw clench on receiving a choice custard pie of an insult, but always he reined in his irritation and sat tight. She admired his restraint. So why was he angry now? Because she had maligned Dee? Because some aspect of the Paris trip worried him? Because she had mocked his sex appeal? Never that. Bottle his charm and the man could make a million. Just a moment ago, when he had been resorting to friendly persuasion, she had been uneasily aware of an increase in the tempo of her heartbeat. And not for the first time, if she was honest. Neille brushed such thoughts aside. Hadn't it been pre-ordained that they meet in the role of antagonists, and thus neutrals?

'You'd like me to keep to heel?' she queried, keeping her tone light.

'That would be preferable to you persistently attempting to show me a clean pair of them. Being civil would also make a welcome change.'

She gave the matter ostentatious thought. 'I dare say that could be arranged.'

'Don't fool around.' Jack was curt. 'I know you aren't going to give in that easily.'

'Have you never wondered if you might have totally the wrong impression about me?' Neille enquired.

'Never.'

'Oh, Jack.' For the second time she ran her finger down the front of his jacket, laughing up at him through inky black lashes. 'You must have realised by now that essentially I'm a girl who's honest and open.' She dug her finger in his ribs. 'As honest and open as you are, zonko.'

Ten minutes later the plane was given clearance to take off and the tension in the cabin began to melt. Once in flight, sandwiches were served and the drinks trolley brought round, and in time the captain reported blue skies at Charles De Gaulle Airport. Jack put aside his brief irritation, and when Neille rummaged in her bag to produce a blood-and-guts thriller, his eyes widened in jokey alarm.

'Don't tell me a sweet young thing like you is an *aficionado*?'

'Guilty,' she grinned. 'Though in defence I should point out I was brainwashed from an early age. Thanks to my cousins, Peter, Paul and Podge, I spent my formative years in mortal fear of doing anything which might remotely be described as feminine.' Neille tapped her fingertips on the paperback. 'I guess something of that's stuck.'

'You were close to your cousins?'

'Very. After all I lived with them in Sussex for thirteen years. It was only after I finished school that I returned to London and my father's house.' She noticed his surprise. 'See, you don't know everything about me,' she said triumphantly.

Jack laughed. 'I know you're not a sissy, that's for sure. So—are you going to fill me in?'

'Provide more facts for that dossier of yours?' she teased.

'If you like.'

Maybe she did like? Even antagonists are allowed to go off-duty sometimes, and fitted into their close-knit weeks had been pleasant patches of relaxation. Jack had proved to be both interesting to listen to, and a good listener.

'My mother died when I was five,' Neille explained, content to leave her book unopened and talk. 'And although I don't remember much about it myself, after her death my father suffered acute depression. Mooie, that's my Aunt Muriel, my mother's sister, arrived one day, decided it was unhealthy for a small child to be cooped up with a brooding man, and whisked me off to stay with her, my Uncle Ken, and their three boys in the country.'

'Didn't you mind?'

'No, I loved it. Throughout her illness my mother had been nursed privately at home, so I was always being warned not to run around, to keep quiet, to be a good little girl. Friends were never allowed in to play. But in Sussex I was free to laugh and shout, and——'

Jack grinned. 'Become a tomboy?'

'Exactly. I was like a puppy let off a leash. Mooie fixed up for me to transfer to the village school and by the time my father was well enough to claim me, I'd become firmly entrenched. I pleaded not to be made to leave, and when he saw the harum-scarum I'd become I suspect the prospect didn't thrill him, either.' Neille laughed. 'He certainly raised no objections when Mooie suggested I become a permanent member of her household, He travelled down to see me at weekends, of course, and we shared holidays together, but Daddy's always found me something of a handful.'

A sardonic brow was raised. 'I wonder why?'

She laughed again. 'I must admit there've been times when I've wondered if I could be a changeling. I'm nothing like my father; nothing like my mother either, so I'm told. She was quiet, demure, shy in company.'

'Did you miss her when she died?'

Neille grew pensive. 'Sad as it sounds, no. She'd been ill for a long time and my only memory is of a pale figure propped up against pillows in a darkened room. She never hugged me or kissed me or swung me round, like Mooie did.' She frowned down at the book, then looked up, teeth worrying her lower lip. 'I was madly jealous of Podge. He's a year younger than me, so we were rivals for a place on Mooie's knee at story time. Whenever we quarrelled Podge always reminded me, with great malicious satisfaction, that she was *his* mother, not mine. It hurt. Funny thing is, it still does.'

Jack was surprised by her disquiet. Surely the girl chewing her lip beside him could not be the same slick miss who was rarely short of an answer? Admissions of vulnerability had not seemed to be Neille's style. Maybe he *did* have the wrong impression about her?

'Your aunt read excerpts from blood-and-guts books?' he enquired, attempting to chase away her melancholy. Neille was tugging strings inside him which hadn't been tugged in a long time, and he found that surprising, too.

'Mooie read boys' stories.' She brightened. 'Biggles *ad nauseam.*'

'Good old Biggles. I had a shelf full.'

'Did you? Do you remember the one about——'

Off they went, swapping memories of childhood books read and re-read over the years. They discovered they had many favourites in common and were still deep in discussion when the plane landed. But conversation had to peter out when, *en masse* with their fellow arrivals, they were directed through the airport's space-age tunnels.

'Suppose I carry the gear while you deal with the red tape?' Jack suggested, as they joined a queue which snaked ahead to the immigration checkpoint. He handed her his passport, and in return humped her tote-bag on to his shoulder. 'What have you got in here—half a hundredweight of eye-shadow?' he asked, pretending to sag at the knees.

'Almost. I thought that as this is my first time in France I'd better fly all flags, so I've come prepared.'

'Your first time? Then I presume you aren't fluent in French?'

'Just the schoolgirl variety,' Neille confessed, wondering why Jack was smiling. 'Communication with the celebrated André could present a problem. If he doesn't speak English it'll need to be sign language.' Waiting in line, she leafed idly through Jack's passport. He was thirty-five years old, six feet two, and well-travelled. 'Identifying mark, scar on left shoulder,' she read out loud and grinned. 'What was that, a stray bullet?' He was on the brink of a reply when Neille gave a trill of laughter. 'Your name's not Jack, it's Jackson. Jackson! Oh, I like that.'

'But I don't,' he said, lips thin. 'So we'll stick with Jack, understand?'

She took no notice. 'Jackson,' she repeated, rolling the name around her mouth. 'Sounds like a butler. Fetch me a mint julep, Jackson,' she quoted plummily, giggling like mad. 'Or a chauffeur. Have the Rolls round at the front portico in two seconds flat and there'll be an extra shilling in your pay packet, Jackson.'

'Bug off.' His eyes were dark and stormy. Vulnerable? He had considered Neille vulnerable? She was as vulnerable as concrete.

'And you.' Her eyes danced. 'Jackson.'

'Nellie.' he retaliated, but the personal high meant she was immune.

'Jackson,' she sang.

'OK, a deal.' He threw down the offer like a hand of bad cards. 'No more Nellie, no more Jackson.'

'We'll see,' she said, as the uniformed *gendarme* in the glass cubicle beckoned them forward. 'We'll see.'

The moment they had been checked and approved, and had moved on, Jack grabbed hold of her arm. 'Yes, we damn well will see,' he hissed. 'You listen to me and you listen good. Make one unilateral move, and you'll suffer. Likewise if you call me Jackson one more time. I've thrown away the kid gloves. From here on in, you get what you deserve. Is that clear?'

'Yes, Jack.'

One other thing shone clear as the sun, now was not the time for a wisecrack. What she had said in the lounge had been true, Jack *was* different and not only in his appearance. He seemed flintier, edgy even. As she made her way beside him across the arrivals hall and out to the taxis, Neille decided there was a streak of tyranny she had never noticed before. But then, he would not be what he was unless he possessed a certain capacity for domination.

'Tell me your plans for the remainder of the day,' he ordered, once the taxi was shooting along the autoroute towards Paris.

Neille checked her watch. 'I had hoped there'd be time for some sightseeing, but now it's too late. I need to prepare myself for tomorrow's photo call.'

'Define "prepare yourself".' His mouth twisted. 'Is that a pseudonym for disappearing off on a jogging jaunt, or do you have an aerobics class fixed in some remote ladies' loo?'

'Neither.' She did her best to sweeten him with one of her wholesome *ingénue* smiles, but Jack remained unmoved. 'I'll be staying in the hotel. Prepare means have a face pack, wax my legs and other sundry tasks. Tomorrow I'm modelling lingerie and one of André's stipulations is that every inch must be smooth and unblemished. Lingerie's a new departure for the fashion house, which makes it vital that these first photographs have an impact. Lingerie's a new departure for me, too,' Neille added, feeling an unwelcome chill of apprehension. 'In my time I've modelled everything from horse blankets to paper dresses, but this is my début into bras and briefs.'

His gaze flickered over her. 'Does Lewis approve?'

'He doesn't know.'

'Shouldn't he?'

'Should he?' she responded, and saw from the abrupt narrowing of his eyes that she had been a shade too defiant. She gave an offhand laugh which was supposed to redress the balance. 'This is the age of topless sunbathing, and girls do appear in night-clubs dotted with little more than six strategically placed sequins. A few shots of me in black lace aren't going to rock anyone back on their heels.'

Jack looked doubtful. 'Not even Lewis?'

'Lewis is just a friend, you know, not my keeper,' she informed him.

'Whatever you call the guy, you have been going out with him for two years,' came the comment, and Neille could not argue with that. 'I agree I only met him for a short time, but it was enough to convince me Lewis Mitchell is a conservative, with a small c.' He paused, choosing his next words with care. 'I'd say he's also acutely conscious of his public image. Don't you think he could get uptight if his girlfriend——'

'Makes like a stripper?' she supplied breezily, hoping to divert him into responding with a quip, but he was stern-faced and intent on making heavy weather.

'Yes. Underwear can be devastatingly see-through these days.' Jack was frowning. 'I presume the photographs will be published in England?'

Neille nodded. 'A week Friday sees the start of a grand advertising campaign in London and simultaneously in other major capitals. This is a rush job, geared to catch the Christmas gift trade. The fashion house has outlets throughout the world, so the exposure will be spread far and wide. It's hard sell.' She neglected to add that she had checked on the timing and range of the campaign before accepting the assignment—or rather, grabbing it with both hands. Prompt and widescale publication of the photographs was of the utmost importance to her. 'Would you become uptight if your girlfriend revealed most, but not all?' she asked, wishing the prospect hadn't suddenly become a screwdriver turning in her stomach.

'That's hypothetical, I'm not Lewis Mitchell,' he replied, showing a stout determination to stay on track. 'I dare say he derives a kick from the media interest generated by his business activities and isn't averse to the odd mention in the gossip columns, as long as it keeps within strict parameters, but you prancing around in next to nothing is . . . something else.'

'Is it?' Neille shrugged with studied indifference. 'Well, that's his problem.'

As Jack dissolved into silence, she gave an inward groan. If only she had been able to make this Paris trip on her own, as originally planned. Arriving in tandem was a definite drawback, but no matter how much she had coaxed, pleaded, grumbled, Jack had refused to be deflected. For her own peace of mind she had wanted to play things discreetly, but now she would be observed. She accepted she would be observed by André, dressers, studio staff, etc., and possibly by the great French public at large, depending on locations, but they were strangers. Jack wasn't a stranger. Not any more. The in-pocket living they had shared meant a closeness had evolved, maybe the erratic, temporary closeness of a warden with his prisoner, but a closeness nonetheless. And an annoying offshoot of this closeness meant that Jack's opinion of her had begun to matter. Dare she take him into her confidence and explain—not the entire motivation in accepting the assignment, of course, but maybe a part? If she censored her tale there would be no harm done, and she would feel easier if he understood.

'You owe Lewis a phone call,' he chastised abruptly, and all thought of taking him into her confidence vanished. Explaining anything to a man who was no more, no less than a bodyguard was reckless in the extreme. Jack was no confidant. His single reason for being with her was money, he had made that plain from the start. And who provided the money? Lewis! Jack's allegiance lay with him, she must never lose sight of that. 'The guy's tried to reach you on several occasions, shouldn't you make the effort to get in touch? Why don't I fix for you to speak to him when I report in?'

'No thanks. I'll get in touch when *I* choose to get in touch,' Neille snapped.

Jack's prompting smacked of the hired help overstepping the mark. He wasn't being paid to chivvy, he was being paid to guard, she thought tetchily. And as he spoke to Lewis every two days, it wasn't as though her 'good friend' didn't know what was happening in her life. Good friend! What a brutal misnomer.

'That sounds high-handed,' Jack replied, continuing to show disapproval. 'I'd be obliged if you'd get in touch soon.'

She bared her teeth at him. 'Yes, sir!'

The hotel *was* discreet, so discreet that, although Dee had claimed it was situated in the fifth *arrondissement*, none of the locals had ever heard of the place. The taxi driver stopped—invariably suddenly and invariably in the middle of the road—and leapt out to brandish the card Jack had provided before passers-by and shopkeepers, but all he received were shakes of heads and Gallic shrugs. Up and down the narrow streets they drove, the taxi driver muttering in despair, until suddenly Neille cried, 'It's there!'

Discreet to the point of fading into oblivion, the hotel entrance was a single varnished door tucked between a *pâtisserie* and a newspaper kiosk. The lobby made no positive statement, either. Furnished in a way which guaranteed instant forgettability, there was an impression of browns— carpet, walls, sofas.

'We have two rooms booked, adjoining,' Jack told the matron who sat knitting behind a desk.

She ran her finger down a list to check their names. *'Ah, oui. Bonjour, monsieur, mais——'* Off she gabbled into crackerjack French, pushing out forms to be filled in, handing over keys to rooms 42 and 43, gesticulating to a beetle-browed man sucking peppermints in a corner, who turned out to be the porter. 'Dinner is served at eight,' she said, making a brief foray into English before returning to her wool and needles.

The porter commandeered their luggage, flung it inside an ancient and minuscule lift, then indicated they must squeeze inside. At a snail's pace they rose skywards, to the accompanying groans of creaking metalwork. No one said a word. The porter, who spent the journey undressing Neille with his eyes, bestirred himself at the fourth floor. Gathering up their suitcases, he marched along the corridor to rooms 42 and 43. He unlocked both doors and, for the first time, directed his attention towards Jack. A tip was expected. A tip was received. Another optical tour of Neille, and he departed.

Jack gestured. 'After you.'

One step inside was enough. 'I've seen bigger cupboards!'

'Perhaps the other room'll be better?' he suggested.

It wasn't. Both were identical brown and beige boxes with tiny *en suite* bathrooms. Space was at a premium. A single bed, one chair and a set of open shelves left nowhere to swing the proverbial cat. The wardrobe consisted of a cubby-hole fitted with a rail and three hangers.

'Thoughtful of them to design the bathroom for midgets,' Neille said antiseptically, discovering that wash-basin, shower and lavatory were jammed together like sardines. She needed room in which to prepare herself. Clear surfaces where her potions and lotions could be stored, a decent mirror, a full-sized bath and a shower which boasted proportions a little more generous than this tiled orange-box.

'As you once told me, don't be picky.' Jack completed a swift reconnoitre. 'Though I must admit the accommodation's not what I had in mind.'

'You don't actually agree that on balance the George V may have a little more going for it?'

He ignored her scorn. 'It's not that. The rooms here are on the compact side, but——'

'Compact!'

'But though they adjoin, they aren't connected— at least, not with each other—with the rooms on either side.' Jack rubbed his chin. 'Do you think that's what the receptionist could have been saying?'

'Probably, but does it matter? The ratfink who

left his nasty messages in Lewis's in-tray isn't about to surface here so I don't need you poised behind a door, ready to fling it wide and rescue me in the nick of time.'

'No?'

'*No.*' Neille knew he'd never revitalise the George V booking and she had not the least intention of abandoning their current resting place in order to trail around Paris searching for suitably adjoining rooms. This hotel was bad enough, but others could be worse. 'I'm one hundred per cent safe here,' she said firmly.

Jack walked over to tap the wall between Numbers 42 and 43. 'This seems thin enough. I guess I'd hear if you did get into trouble.'

'I won't!' She crawled across the bed to the window—the only way to reach it—and eased open the catch. She looked out, turning to flash a plastic smile over her shoulder. 'What a wonderful panorama! Do come and share it with me.'

He clambered to join her and together they surveyed the view. Opposite, only a stone's throw away, were office windows where three typists gazed balefully back from behind their typewriters. Look up, to avoid the typists, and you saw grey slate roofs and a small patch of sky. Look down, to avoid the typists, and there was a courtyard where a single tree, at present leafless, struggled for survival. In one corner dustbins spilled more garbage than they held. In another was looped a washing line, naked apart from an ample supply of garish pegs. As their eyes were being drawn magnetically back to meet those of the typists, an invisible clarinettist began to play a doleful lament.

'Paris offers something for everyone,' Neille said, closing the window. 'Eyes across a godforsaken courtyard and all night clarinet concertos.'

'How do you know the clarinet's going to play all night?' Jack asked, as he backed off the bed.

'How do you know it won't?'

'Come on, it's not that bad,' he coaxed. 'Like Dee promised, the hotel's——'

'Clean and comfortable? Didn't she do us proud? Why not drop her a postcard and tell her there are doves on the roof? She'll be thrilled.'

He eyed her with wry tolerance. 'Have you ever considered going into a nunnery? One where the novices take a vow of silence?' He stepped aside to avoid any blows he might have provoked, which meant he was standing by the door. 'I agree this place isn't the George V, but I'm afraid you'll just have to accept it.'

'Why should I?' Neille muttered, as he departed. Why did she have to accept his decisions? She unlocked her suitcase and fitted what clothes she could on to the three hangers. The remainder had to be crammed on to the shelves with her shoes. Suddenly she tilted her head to one side, and listened. The walls *were* thin, she could hear a shower running in Room 42. She grinned—a wide, triumphant grin. After three long weeks, her time had come. So much for keeping to heel, so much for waxing her legs. She was going out for a walk—alone!

Wary of using the creaky lift, Neille crept down the four flights of stairs, crossed the lobby and exited at speed. Hands in the pockets of her parka, white-trousered legs set apart, booted feet on the pavement, she took a deep breath of fresh French air. She had done it! Freedom at last! Excitement at having got the better of her constant companion bubbled. Now at liberty to do exactly as she pleased, she could thumb her nose at the clever Mr Jack Rea—and at Lewis!

She would explore, though she must be careful not to go too far. A short unaccompanied stroll was one thing, a precipitate rush into the rabbit-warren streets of a foreign city would be another. Neille looked uphill to a crossroads, then downhill to a cobbled square. The square seemed interesting. Unable to detach her grin, she sauntered slowly down. The shops she passed were intriguingly Parisian. A window filled with gold-lacquered antiques first captured her attention, then a quaint booth selling chocolate truffles. She stood for ages outside an art shop where a panoply of oil paintings was displayed. One, an abstract of what appeared to be a hedgehog with a feather, sported a price tag of over fifty thousand francs, expensive in any language. Jack would've had something to say about that!

Reaching the square, Neille sat on a bench to watch the world eddy around her. It was amazing how a short flight, a mere twenty-one miles of intervening ocean, made such a difference. The people were darker, grainier, noisier. The traffic which poured in and out of the square was different, too. Almost every single vehicle sported battle scars, and it was easy to see why. Renaults cut corners, Peugeots charged up kerbs, battered Citroëns performed like crazed rams, banging and barging. And in the midst of it all, on a podium, stood a *gendarme* in a white coat. He was directing the traffic like a lunatic conductor in charge of a homicidal orchestra.

Neille was fascinated, and only the chill of approaching dusk and the increasing frequency of gummy smiles from a gnarled old man who had joined her on the bench, brought an end to her furlough. She tramped back up the hill, thinking how Jack would have enjoyed watching the people and the traffic. What would his comment have been on the hedgehog picture? She must tell him about that. Neille strode across the hotel lobby and into the lift. As she rammed the gate shut, she decided to tell him nothing. She had never intended to keep her excursion a secret, indeed half the fun had been the prospect of being able to gloat, but suddenly it struck her that this itch to tell him was akin to dependency. He was becoming a habit. Would she miss him next week? With irritating honesty, she admitted she would. After all, he had been with her virtually twenty-four hours a day for what was beginning to seem like forever.

She had stepped from the lift at the fourth floor, and was walking along the corridor, when she heard an intake of breath. With a jolt, Neille realised Jack was waiting. Even in the gloom it was plain to see how he bristled with fury, like a predatory beast ready to pounce.

'And where have you been?' he demanded.

'Out.' With a defiant flourish, she unlocked the door to her room. 'I don't live by your rules, Jackson, so I fail to see what——'

'Your lesson for today,' he growled, 'is that my rules are the *only* rules.' One step, and he pressed his hand into the small of her back and thrust her into the room. A backward kick shut the door. Clutching her in a wrestling type hold, he more or less fell with her on to the bed, where he positioned her across his knees. 'Now,' he said, holding her firm. 'How would you like your bottom to be spanked—hard, harder or hardest?'

Winded and face down, Neille needed a moment or two to recover. She twisted her head around to glare, her hair tumbling into her eyes.

'You wouldn't dare.'

'Wouldn't I?' A large hand was ominously raised.

'Arghh!' she shrieked, kicking and struggling for all she was worth. 'Let me go!' It never occurred to her to think what the other guests might make of the noise.

'Like hell. I'm sick and tired of being treated as your stooge. From now on, we do things my way.'

'I wouldn't bet on that, Jackson,' she retaliated.

He was being too Neanderthal for words. How dare he threaten to paddywack her and sling her across his knees like a sack of coal? She had never been so offended, so humiliated. Peter, Paul and Podge may have stuffed worms down her neck, made apple-pie beds, even suspended her head-down over a cow-pat, but then she had been a child. For her, a grown woman, to be on the brink of having her backside paddled represented degradation of the highest degree. But in addition to degradation she was aware of another sneaky feeling—arousal. It was disgusting! The way Jack was manhandling her had set off a raw sexual buzz. Neille was furious with herself. How could she simultaneously feel degraded, yet intimately aware? And suppose he decided to yank down her trousers or even the scrap of white silk she called 'knickers' and administer a full scale thrashing? She would die if he slapped her bare buttocks.

'You louse! You beast! You——' She fought, panting and pawing, but it was no use. One hand pressed down on her spine, Jack used the other to disastrous effect. Thwack! Her posterior tingled. It was unfortunate her blood was tingling, too. 'I'll report you to Lewis,' she cried.

'Is that the best you can come up with?' He laughed grimly. 'Lewis is on my side. He'd agree that this is long overdue. For three damned weeks you've been trying to drive me into a frenzy— well, now you've succeeded. And don't call me Jackson!' His hand was raised. 'Want another one?'

'No, no! Please don't slap me again,' she begged. Neille had just remembered something. 'Tomorrow I'm to be photographed in underwear, so I mustn't be bruised.'

'You don't want to appear technicoloured, black and blue?'

'No way.' Fear of another thwack had her ricocheting from appeals to aggression. 'You wouldn't do this to me if I was a man.'

'Damned right, I wouldn't. I'd probably knock you out cold.'

'But you're supposed to be *protecting* me from violence, not inflicting it,' she yelled, as his hand stiffened in mid-air. 'Jack, I'll behave. I'll never go anywhere without you again,' she gurgled. 'Honest.'

'Honest? You, honest? If I believe that I'll believe anything,' he said, but he relented, shoving her unceremoniously off his knee on to the bed. 'I guess you're right, corporal punishment isn't the answer. And I am here to ensure no one lays a finger on you.' He sighed, wryly shaking his head. 'I consider myself civilised, but somehow you bring out my baser instincts.' He gave a suddenly ferocious glare. '*All* of them.'

Pink-faced, Neille scrambled to her feet. 'I'm sorry. I agree my behaviour hasn't been exactly . . . perfect.'

'Perfect!' He rolled his eyes.

'And I realise now I should never have gone out alone.'

'No, you shouldn't.' Jack thrust a thumb into his chest. 'Because this joker is accountable for your safety. I'm well aware that three weeks ago you made up your mind, without thought or hesitation, that the note Lewis received was sterile, but an element of danger can't be discounted.'

'Can't it?' Try as she might, she could not prevent disbelief from entering her tone.

He gave a grunt of impatience. 'I reckon the only way to get it into your thick head is to give you all the facts. When Lewis found the note, a newspaper cutting was attached—a photograph of the pair of you at some antiques fair.'

'A photograph of me?' Neille had been rubbing her backside, but now she paused. 'Why didn't someone say something?'

'Because, in his wisdom, your father insisted you weren't to be worried. He even managed to persuade the police not to interview you. How's that for irony. Your father's shredded with nerves, while you don't give a damn.'

'You think I should?' She had become subdued. This information altered the entire scenario.

'It's always common sense to be on the alert,' Jack replied, using a voice which made her wonder about the rank he had held in the SAS. Captain? It would have been a position of authority.

'But,' she began, wrinkling her nose, 'I still don't——'

'Enough!' An awesome hand chopped through the air. 'Consider the matter closed. I'm finished with you and your perpetual arguments. Why is it you always beg to differ?' Jack was at the door, wrenching it open. 'You and I will eat dinner in the restaurant downstairs at eight p.m. precisely, until which time you are to remain in this room. After dinner you return and stay put until morning. I'll collect you for breakfast at seven-thirty. And that, Neille Trenchard, is that!'

CHAPTER FOUR

AT breakfast Jack continued to treat her with concise disdain, becoming the spare-of-words, sure-of-shot hulk she had once visualised. Maybe a sweat-stained vest did lurk beneath his jersey? Maybe he did strike matches on his jeans zip as a party piece? Hoping to make amends, she tried to soften his mood with smiles and small talk, but he refused all overtures. Neille had seen friendlier faces behind riot shields.

One part of her didn't blame him. His annoyance had been a long time building and his grievances were genuine. He was entitled to keep her in the doghouse—hadn't her behaviour been that of a bitch? But another part of Neille felt vexed, betrayed even. Jack had always shown such patience and good humour, did he have to extend this 'sit—don't move—stay' treatment? What must she do to merit a pat on the head? Sit up and beg? If so, Jack had picked the wrong girl. Neille stopped smiling and talking, and retreated. He had distanced himself from her and two could play at that game. Why should she concern herself with a man who had pummelled her physically, and who now seemed intent on pummelling her emotionally?

She switched her mind to other matters. He had spoken of danger, but where? She refused to panic and interpret the inclusion of her photograph as a personal threat, especially at this late stage. She glanced around the cellar restaurant. Their fellow guests looked stolidly normal: middle-aged French couples, in the main, with a sprinkling of overseas visitors. No assassins here. Danger? Phooey! Hadn't three uneventful weeks passed by since note and photograph had landed on Lewis's desk? Not exactly uneventful, she decided, sneaking a look at the man on the other side of the table. Life with Jack could never be described as that. Neille snapped her mind back to the note. Photograph or not, she didn't accept threats from anyone—not from the nasty little person who had written those nasty little words, nor from Jack. Jack again! She had suffered no after-effects from having her backside thwacked—a head-over-the-shoulder peer into the mirror had shown she was completely unmarked—but lack of bruises did not mean she was prepared to forgive and forget. Not now. Not when Jack refused forgiveness for *her* past sins.

'Shall we take the Métro to André's studio?' Neille suggested, as they walked out of the hotel. Legs waxed, skin toned, eyes bright and shining, she was ready to go. André possessed a formidable reputation, and whether modelling lingerie or not the assignment was something of a scoop. If only that screwdiver wouldn't turn inside her whenever she thought about removing her clothes. 'I've worked out the route on the map,' she continued, 'and it looks easy. The studio's on the Right Bank, almost next door to a Métro station and——' She pointed up the hill to where a huge orange M indicated access. '—we can board a direct line from there.'

Jack eyed the traffic which was filling the street with engine noise and fumes. 'I dare say the Métro could be preferable to getting snarled up among this lot,' he acquiesced. 'Especially as it'd probably take us ages to find a taxi in the first place.'

'Then the Métro it is. Come on. I promise not to get us lost.'

They joined a band of commuters in a headlong rush down numerous flights of stone steps into the bowels of the earth.

'I'll get the tickets,' Jack offered when they reached the subterranean booking offices, and Neille was grateful. It was the morning rush hour, and bedlam. The queue—queue!—was a scrum where you were in danger of being tackled in a manner which would have guaranteed cries of ecstasy from the French Rugby Federation. When he returned, holding aloft two pieces of yellow card, he allowed her the first smile of the day. 'How's that for service?' he demanded.

Through the barriers, the pace increased. People elbowed, prodded, cursed their way along the corridors. Fall, and you'd have been trampled underfoot. Travellers barged past, clattered down steps like automatons, thrust everyone else aside. The old and infirm did not stand a chance. Keeping a sharp look out for the correct route colour, Neille acted as navigator and successfully, if breathlessly, brought them to the appropriate platform. A train was just pulling in. One gasp for oxygen, and they were stampeded inside.

'Phew!' she exclaimed, as Jack smacked up against her.

He looked around the crowded carriage where there was not an inch to spare. 'You call this easy? Next time we go difficult. We go by taxi.'

Neille managed to squeeze a hand up between their bodies to touch her brow. 'Yes, sir.'

Her humour emerged a trifle shaky. Being pressed up against Jack was disturbing. He was annoyingly *male*. All animal, as Dominic had said. This man throbbed with good red blood and muscle, energised by a discreet, yet powerful, sexuality. Not like Lewis, whose layers of urbanity often made her wonder if he was generated by nothing more than a microchip. When the train set off, Neille clung on to the strap of her tote-bag with both hands and tried to ignore the male chest, pelvis and legs which were being joggled against hers. An attempt to shift her stance resulted in being nudged back in place by surrounding commuters, so there seemed no way to avoid him. She would have expected a vapid female like Dee to turn pink and coy at this body contact, but not her. Yet her pulse-rate had accelerated, and the heat she felt rising could not be wholly attributed to the packed compartment.

When stations came and went, and the crowd began to thin, she was grateful. No longer pressed up against him, Neille felt sturdier. At a mainline station there was a decided exit, and she was able to sit down. When another seat came free further down the carriage, Jack walked off to make claim.

'Give me the nod when we're due to exit,' he instructed.

Taking out her guidebook, Neille rechecked the route. In actual fact, the photographer's studio was positioned half-way between two stations. She had given Jack the name of the second, but there was no reason why they shouldn't surface at the first. The stations were close together, there would be nothing in the distance. A slow grin built on her mouth. Yesterday's assurance that she would behave had been extracted under duress, which rendered it null and void. And as long as he continued to treat her like a disobedient mutt which he was attempting to train, there was the temptation to behave that way. Neille mulled over the idea. It might work. She would make it work.

Ten yards away, her companion was growing restless. He had guessed they must be nearing their destination, and when they pulled into the next stop he looked up expectantly. She shook her head. The carriage doors slid open to allow passengers to depart, passengers to file on. She saw Jack stretch, yawn, lean back his head and rub his eyes. As the doors started to close, Neille leapt up. She whistled through the gap and landed with a thump on the platform. There was only time to glimpse an astonished Jack rising from his seat in the departing train, before she turned and ran. Tote-bag banging against her hip, Neille pounded up the stairs. It was impossible to contain her glee, and her burst of laughter had other commuters turning around to gape. She ran along the corridors, not knowing why running mattered when he wouldn't, couldn't follow, only knowing that running comprised a vital ingredient. Her escape was like something out of *Boy's Own*. Trenchard strikes again! Hee, hee!

It was only when she reached the final flight of steps that she slowed to walking pace; then she was free to step out on to the busy Paris street. Cold air slapped her face, but the zing of blood in her veins meant Neille did not notice. Her evasion of Jack might only be temporary, yet it was

enough. She had proved her superiority. Hee, hee
again! It could well take him two hours or more to
trace her because, even if he had memorised
André's address, his inadequate French guaranteed
he'd hit a few snags. Great! And if he punished her
again—well, this freedom gesture was worth it.
Consulting the guidebook, Neille worked out the
path to the studio and set off, hips swinging in
delight. She turned a corner. Hee, hee! How clever
she was. She turned another, passing flower shops
where roses and carnations were arranged with
a natural flair for colour. Not merely clever—
brilliant!

'Gotcha!'

A heavy hand landed on her shoulder and Neille
almost jumped out of her skin. When she jerked
her head around, her blue eyes grew to the size of
saucers. Clever? Brilliant? Here was Jack. He was
panting, his broad chest rising and falling beneath
the leather jacket.

'How—how have you found me?' she asked,
uncertain whether she should be furious or lost in
admiration. When he remained silent, catching his
breath, her imagination took over. 'Did you pull
the emergency cord and stop the train?'

'No,' he gasped. 'I jumped off at the next station
and ran back.'

'Ran back? Along the line? Through the tunnel?'
He nodded, and she gazed at him in horror.
Images flashed through her mind. A train mowing
him down. Jack being flung into the air or sliced
limb from torso. Going up in a puff of smoke if
he'd stumbled against a live electric cable. And she
had made him take these chances! Her escape
attempt now seemed frivolous and shallow, ill-

considered in the extreme. 'But only an idiot would run along a railway line,' she protested feebly.

'Only an idiot did.'

Neille felt dreadful. 'You could have been maimed or——' Her voice trailed into silence as her thoughts preoccupied her. 'How did you know which way I'd gone when you came up on to the street?'

'I——' He spoke on an outgoing breath. 'I bugged you.'

'Bugged me?' After a moment it sank in. 'Bugged me!' she shrieked.

'In there.' He nodded at the tote-bag on her shoulder. 'Don't worry about it now,' Jack said, when she ripped open the drawstring and began scrabbling her hands through a conglomeration of lipsticks and blushers, scarves, tights and brushes. 'I'll remove the bug this evening, when we're back at the hotel.'

'But I *do* worry.' Her look scorched him. Maybe she wasn't to blame for him living dangerously. Hadn't the do-or-die response been all his own? 'How dare you bug me?'

'How dare you continually challenge my credibility?' enquired Jack, lobbing home an equaliser.

With compressed lips, Neille fastened her tote-bag. She had not found the bug, did not even have much idea what she was supposed to be looking for, and now there seemed nothing else to do except continue on her way.

'So, what happens?' she asked, as he walked alongside, yet again. 'Another assault on my posterior?'

He produced a curt laugh. 'Physical contact's too risky.'

'Is it?' she asked, dry mouthed, as she jumped to the conclusion that Jack, too, had been aware of that sexual buzz. But he hadn't, his next words proved it.

'Yeah. I said if you'd been a man I'd have knocked you out cold and, believe me, only by exercising the greatest restraint did I manage to keep from throwing a left hook yesterday. If I lay my hands on you a second time it might well result in murder, and I've no intention of growing old in a French jail on your behalf.' She received a strafing glance. 'This time your punishment will be—subtle.'

'How—subtle?' Neille enquired, feeling itchy. She might have outwitted him just now, but for no more than a few minutes. And her success, if it could be counted as a success, was only the second in three weeks of determined trying.

'Wait and see.' His eyes were mean as back streets. 'But you can be sure of one thing. Whatever it takes, you will pay.'

Minutes later he delivered her into the custody of André, a butch character in creased dungarees, and departed; though not before making certain she would not be released until late afternoon at the earliest. Whether Jack had secreted himself in a cubbyhole within shouting distance, or gone for a stroll along the Champs-Elysées, she had no idea. One thing she did know: wherever he was, he would be planning his revenge. What form would it take?

Luckily André spoke English, if heavily accented English. He introduced her to her partners, two aloof French brunetttes with short spiky hair like frozen dishmops, and then explained the programme which lay ahead. Today, shots taken would be featured as advertisements in magazines and newspapers. Tomorrow they would leave the studio and go on location around Paris, capturing publicity stills for circulation amongst women's page editors. Thursday and Friday, there would be run-of-the-mill poses for the fashion house's own catalogue.

During the two hours in which she had her hair frizzed into a fashionably shaggy style, her face painted, her body poured into sugar-pink corsets and out of silver stretch mini-slips, she constantly fretted about Jack's threatened revenge. Only when André lined her up with the brunettes before a shimmering backdrop did she abandon the subject. But she rapidly realised all she had done was swap one unease for another.

'Zee boobs oop, *chérie*,' ordered André, wind-milling wiry arms and exposing tufts of black hair in the process.

Neille had never considered herself voluptuous, but alongside the emaciated Parisiennes she became so. She felt unbelievably womanly, Rubensesque even with her clouds of copper-gold hair and her curves. She attempted to perform a balancing act between the chaste and the provoca-tive but wondered if, on this occasion, she could be accused of playing the tramp? The silk of the camiknickers she wore was fine, erring on the sheer. She told herself she was being a prude, and tried to remember topless sunbathing and sequinned girls in night-clubs, but it didn't work. Pouting at the camera in a state of undress felt *sleazy*. This wasn't a fun thing. Perhaps she would have felt different if it was? But the assignment had been undertaken as yet another attempt to solve a problem, and time was running out. Neille shivered. An added worry was the thought of her father's dismay when she appeared semi-clad in the newspapers. Poor Daddy. Here she was, distressing him again. Yet his precarious calm had to be sacrificed, what alternative was there? And short-term *malaise* was surely a small price to pay in return for the long-term survival of his peace of mind? If her ploy worked—*if*.

Her outfits were changed throughout the day, but the jitters remained a constant factor. André proved to be both perfectionist and dictator. A hair out of place created ructions, a négligé which fell awkwardly had him bellowing. A bevy of helpers scuttled around, but they never did the right thing, and as the sky darkened and the lights came on all over Paris, so pressure-cooker steam built up. Neille's head throbbed with the photographer's constant shouting, her back ached from being stretched in bizarre poses, and her smile had began to settle into a gargoyle grimace. And *still* she felt tarty. The only thing to be thankful for was that Jack had steered clear. His witnessing of her discomfort would have been too much to bear.

At last André threw up his hands in despair at having been saddled with morons, and the photo session was over. Neille hobbled off to the dressing room, but was only allowed one gesture of commiseration from the brunettes before being ignored. Chattering away in French, they never so much as glanced her way. But they glanced Jack's way when he knocked at the door fifteen minutes later.

'I want,' he said, poking his head into the room. 'I want Neille.' He found her, face creamed clean and fully dressed, tugging on her boots.

'You wouldn't prefer either of us?' enquired one of the brunettes, wobbling her head in a very French way. Without warning, she could speak English. Odd, when previously she had never uttered a word. 'You wouldn't prefer a local girl to introduce you to the *ooh-là-lá?*'

'Tempting, but I must refuse.' Amusement gave him a very sexy smile. 'Neille here demands all my attention.'

The other girl spoke up. 'You are Neille's *amant?*'

Jack draped himself in the doorway. 'I guess you could say that.'

'No, you couldn't!' Intent on objection, Neille marched forward, but as she neared him an arm snaked out and she found herself fitted as snugly into his body as she had been on the Métro. 'Jack,' she protested, '*amant* means——'

'Lover.' He bent and spoke into her ear. 'For the remainder of our time together, sunbeam, I am to be your *amant*, boyfriend, call it what you will. Courtesy of Lewis.'

'Whatever are you talking about?' she enquired, aware of the brunettes sitting up and taking notice of what must appear to be a fond *tête-à-tête*.

'Romance.' He looked across to their audience and winked. 'Isn't that what Paris is about? Stolen kisses, tenderness, a hand on a naked thigh?'

As the girls giggled, Neille gazed at him in alarm. He was implying they had been, and would be, intimate. Didn't both brunettes have that look of 'aha' in their eyes? Too late to claim innocence, the damage had been done. Jack had taken her into a hug, said a few choice words, and effectively labelled her as his. She felt—what did she feel? Annoyed with his trickery, she supposed, yet contrarily pleased because the hoity-toity French girls were so obviously impressed. Their male counterparts had a reputation for being virile lovers, but this tall Englishman had been placed in the same category. And Jack was playing the role to perfection.

'Excuse us, ladies, now we're off to find oysters and champagne, and maybe later——' He lifted her tote-bag on to his shoulder. '—gentle lamplight and horizontal bliss. *Au revoir.*'

'*Au revoir,*' breathed both brunettes.

'Oysters and champagne?' Neille queried, as he led her out of the studio, down the stairs, and on to the street. 'Lamplight and horizontal bliss?'

Paris by night, with its glittering shops and illuminated palaces, was the stuff of which dreams are made, but she was too intent on questioning Jack to notice.

'Poetic licence,' he replied.

'You're damned right!' Neille had to almost run to keep up, for he had hold of her hand and was taking her with him across a beautiful square adorned with stone sculptures. Fountains rose like silver plumes in the moonlight. They had reached the far side of the square before it struck her how his hand felt big and warm and *right*. It shouldn't. Weren't they antagonists? Wasn't theirs a strictly business and neutral relationship? She wasn't prepared for anything else. And up until yesterday when—her cheeks grew hot in remembrance—he had tanned her hide, there hadn't been anything

else. Was there now? All Jack was doing was
holding her hand in a random kind of way.
Random to him, maybe, but not to her. Neille was
tempted to pull free, yet didn't, scared he might
realise how much his hand-clasp disturbed her. If
he suspected her of a weakness, especially such a
frivolous, feminine weakness, might he not exploit
it for all he was worth? 'I'd be grateful if you'd
explain,' she puffed, when he stopped outside a
red-canopied *brasserie.* 'What do you mean, you're
to be my——' She chose the lesser of the two evils.
'—boyfriend?'

She received no reply, for Jack had more
pressing matters on his mind. 'I presume you're
hungry?' he asked.

'Yes, but——'

'Then we'll eat.' He ushered her forward up
the steps and into the restaurant. Cartwheel
chandeliers hung from the ceiling, and the décor
was of rich dark wood and brass. A waiter,
officious as a penguin, marched up and led them
to a discreet booth. Menus were distributed, then
the waiter produced pencil and notepad. He
waited, regally impatient. 'We'd like time to
decide,' Jack requested, and with a sniff the man
walked away.

All that had passed Neille's lips since breakfast
were two cups of coffee, so the sight and smell of
well-cooked food instantly made her mouth water.
The menu offered a selection of *entrées, poissons,
les viandes grillées ou rôties* and *les mets
gourmands*, which required a valiant stab at
translation.

'Madame?'

The waiter had returned, thin, dark and prone to

pomposity. That they had dared to enter his shrine had clearly caused offence.

'This, please,' said Neille, poking her finger at the list.

He sniffed his disapproval. *'Et monsieur?'*

In an atrocious accent Jack ordered fresh salmon with butter sauce. 'And a bottle of white wine,' he added. 'A good one.'

'You think we serve anything else?' the waiter demanded, and strutted off.

Jack laughed. 'How can Paris be so damned splendid and the Parisians so damned awful?'

'They can't all be the same.' She grinned. 'Can they?' Ready to follow on with a comment about the behaviour of the two French models, Neille suddenly stiffened. After a tension-packed day it was tempting to relax and go plop, but there was a matter of some importance to be cleared up first. 'I'm still waiting for an explanation,' she reminded him, switching to stone-faced school ma'am. 'What's this about Lewis agreeing to you being my—boyfriend?'

Jacket sloughed off and sweater sleeves pushed up to reveal strong forearms, Jack was smiling. 'You aren't the only one who was busy today,' he told her, clasping his hands loosely behind his head and tilting back his chair. 'I made a number of phone calls, one of which was to Lewis. I reported how you'd become increasingly frisky of late.'

Her chin lifted. 'You admitted you'd lost me?'

'I did.' There was a momentary hang-dog expression before his smile returned. 'I then told him how losing you had alerted me to the fact that I was hampered in my role of bodyguard. That in my opinion it was time to . . . move in.'

'Move in?' Neille didn't care for the sound of that.

There was a pause as the waiter appeared with the wine. He uncorked it between his knees and poured Jack an inch in his glass for tasting.

'It's smarter if I'm not blatantly on surveillance,' he said, nodding approval which enabled both glasses to be filled before the waiter stalked away. 'As our present arrangement stands, any villain would immediately recognise me as an outsider. That leaves you wide open.'

'How?' she enquired cagily.

'If I'm parked six feet away, I'd be unable to deflect a knife which is wielded at three.'

Neille sat up straighter. 'You want us to be glued together?'

At that moment the waiter returned and plonked down two plates. Jack's salmon, accompanied by boiled potatoes and broccoli, looked appetising, but Neille viewed her plate with wary eyes. Was this the *nouvelle cuisine* had she read about? She had never expected a fan-shaped arrangement of pale meat in a brown sauce. Chopped mushrooms sat to one side, while a heap of what could only be mashed swede was on the other.

Jack made a finger and thumb loop of excellence, and began to eat. 'Not exactly glued,' he said, once he'd filled himself up sufficiently to be able to afford a break. 'But closer in public.'

'I don't see why that's necessary, especially not after all this time,' she protested. She wished he would stop talking about moving in and getting closer. The words themselves were potent enough to send the blood rushing to her head, she dreaded to think what might happen if the words ever became actions. 'The danger—if there is danger—

hasn't increased,' Neille continued. 'Don't forget that come next Monday I'll be out in the big wide world all on my own.'

All on her own. Why did that sound like an anti-climax?

'I haven't forgotten, sunbeam, but as a response to your love of truancy I had no option but to undertake a radical rethink.' Jack broke off to make another onslaught on his salmon. 'It became clear to me that the screws must be tightened. As I explained to Lewis, any villain would be suspicious of a bodyguard, yet undeterred by a——'

'Boyfriend,' Neille provided, when he paused.

His grey eyes crinkled. 'You got it in one. More wine?'

'Please,' she said, surprised to discover her glass was empty.

'Allowed perfection, our villain would leap in believing I'm no threat at all and then be overpowered.' He noticed how she had not yet begun to eat. 'I thought you were hungry.'

'I am.' She filled her fork. The meat tasted like solid chicken, and required to be washed down with a mouthful of wine. 'All this talk of villains leaping and you overpowering makes me wonder if you've seen too many episodes of Batman and Robin,' she said drily.

'Could be.' His smile was ingenuous. 'Whatever, until we go our separate ways I am officially——' The way he paused made her scowl, '——your boyfriend.'

'And Lewis agreed to this?'

'Gave me *carte blanche*. Please feel free to ring him and verify.'

'No thanks.' Neille abandoned the meat to make a start on the mushrooms. Thankfully they were normal. 'Verification's the last thing I need. It doesn't surprise me in the least that the two of you have gone behind my back and fixed things, once again.'

'For your own safety, sunbeam, for your own safety,' he assured her solemnly, but there was a gleam in his eye.

'I bet! This radical rethink is just you getting even.' She glowered for a moment, then asked haughtily, 'Aren't you forgetting something? It takes two to be——' The word needed to be pushed out, '—lovers. And I have not the slightest intention of pretending to be in love with you.'

'Maybe you'll discover you like it?'

'Maybe I won't. A bodyguard you are, and a bodyguard you'll stay.'

Jack shrugged amiably. 'Aren't you going to eat that meat?' Neille shook her head. 'Then shall I?'

'Make yourself at home,' she muttered.

He grinned as he leant forward to help himself from her plate. 'Don't worry, I intend to.'

A double-edged comment if she had ever heard one! In threatening to move in closer, Jack had located her weak spot with dispiriting ease. For two years she had lived in an uncomplicated emotional vacuum which suited her fine, but now this carnivorous cowboy was galloping in, pennant fluttering in the breeze. Her nerves jangled. Had he guessed she did not find him entirely unattractive and intended to take a ride at her expense? Well, think again, Jack!

'A public charade is pointless, and especially

here in Paris,' she insisted. 'Any villain will have stayed at h0me. He'd never have bothered to cross the Channel.'

'So spake the oracle.' He laid down his knife and fork. 'Neille, the way in which I make my living is security, and right now I happen to be looking out for you. If I consider I can be more effective closer, then closer I will be.'

Jack started to eat again, leaving her to accept she had been out-classed, out-pointed, and only had herself to blame. If she had behaved, the bodyguard relationship would have been maintained. Now anything might happen. 'Moving in' sounded nail-bitingly ambiguous. What did Jack intend to do? There was no point asking him to spell it out; keeping her guessing would be an integral part of his game. And to him it *was* a game. From the occasional comments he had made about his past, it was obvious he had never been troubled by a shortage of feminine company. Kissing and cuddling would be second nature. Suppose he decided to kiss and cuddle her? Jack's sexual fire-power promised to be impressive. Once intimacy had been no problem, but ever since Simon's death she had shied away. When she did fall in love again she had promised herself it would be the real thing, devout and lifelong, not just a brief dizzy spurt. Love? Where did love fit into this? She was not making sense. At most Jack would kiss her. A kiss wasn't much. She was panicking without reason.

'Enjoy my meat?' she enquired sweetly. 'And my swede?'

'Very tasty,' he grinned, wiping his mouth on a napkin. 'I presume that was the *Cul de Lapin?*'

'I'm afraid so. I didn't mean to order it, I thought I'd asked for fillet steak.'

'Desserts?' barked the waiter, bending over them.

Neille chose a calorific Bombe Alaska, followed by coffee. Jack just had coffee.

'There's really no need for you to hang around and watch me in action with André tomorrow,' she said, spooning in meringue. She had attempted a flippant tone, but heard it fall flat. 'Your dash along the Métro this morning has put me clean off escape attempts. But that apart, I'm not going to do a bunk mid-session, am I?'

Jack looked her straight in the eye. 'What's the matter?' he enquired. 'Don't you want me to see you in your underwear?'

'Um, no—no, it's not that,' she stammered. On the first evening they had met he had said something about climbing into people's minds and now, to her confusion, he had climbed right into hers! He could never have guessed how much today's modelling had upset her, could he? 'It—standing by all day seems a waste of your time,' Neille finished weakly.

'Haven't you been listening, sunbeam? I'm moving in. Which means I shall be there tomorrow, watching you every minute of the day.' His grin was mischievous. 'Shouldn't be too onerous. You have a great body and an especially tantalising backside.'

'Thanks,' she smiled, then straight away cursed herself for responding. She must remember that from now on every single thing Jack said or did was suspect.

'By the way,' he said. 'Can you translate *lapin*?'

'Rabbit.'

'What!' He had been drinking coffee, but now he slammed down his cup, setting the saucer awash. He stared at her aghast. 'Rabbit? But I thought it was beef or veal or something. Rabbit? I've eaten rabbit? But I had a pet rabbit when I was a kid. He was called Snowy, and was big and white and cuddly. I used to rub my cheek up against his fur. And now—oh, God! I've eaten one.'

His dismay restored her in an instant, and Neille giggled.

'Just goes to prove that crime—stealing off my plate—never pays.' She was on the brink of adding 'zonko', but decided it was wiser to refrain. From now on she must tread carefully. 'May I ask the waiter to bring you another dish?' she enquired. 'Why not try a few frogs' legs or a plate of snails?'

Jack held his stomach. 'Don't,' he groaned.

Looking pained, he settled the bill and led Neille out into the night. When he reached for her hand, she made no protest. Although the gesture had appeared automatic, she was not fooled. Holding her hand was a part of Jack's plan. Well, she would show him she didn't care. Maybe if he felt 'moving in' was having little effect, he would 'move out'? Besides, his hand was warm and comforting, and if passers-by were glancing at them, marking them down as yet another pair of lovers, being coupled in public with Jack was by far preferable to being coupled with Lewis.

By the time they reached the hotel he had recovered.

'How about a nightcap?' he suggested. 'It would make a pleasant end to the——'

'No thanks.' Cutting him off in mid-sentence, Neille darted for the lift. There was something in his grin which she didn't trust. In addition to a nightcap, was he lining up a kiss as another pleasant end to the evening? Did he intend to enfold her in an embrace? It was the indecision which killed, not knowing which way he'd jump. 'Alcohol makes wrinkles,' she said pretentiously, 'and I need an early night. But you go ahead. See you tomorrow.'

'Until tomorrow,' he agreed, smiling as she rose slowly skywards.

Tomorrow will be different, Neille told herself as she undressed. By tomorrow she would have grown a second skin and become blasée. She would. She would! Eight hours' sleep was necessary to maintain her dewy look, but sleep refused to come. Later, when the door to Room 42 was unlocked, her ears pricked up of their own accord. Jack was moving around, and then he began to whistle. The tune sounded vaguely familiar. What was it? A children's song? Then she recognised the lilt. He was whistling 'Nellie the Elephant'!

CHAPTER FIVE

THE two great stone towers of Notre Dame stood high and proud against a clear blue sky. Built many centuries ago, the Gothic cathedral continued to inspire awe in the visitors who travelled from all parts of the world to pay homage, but this morning there was an added attraction. A mobile caravan had been parked alongside the Place du Parvis, the large square in front of the cathedral, and it was apparent from the frenzied comings and goings that this did duty as an operations centre. A portion of the square had been cordoned off, and here tripods and arc lamps were being assembled. Long lengths of cable appeared. André, as domineering as ever, shouted instructions, countermanded them, regurgitated the original request. Tourists began to gather in knots, discussing among themselves what all the fuss could be about.

When Neille stepped down from the caravan, there was a sudden hush. The tourists gaped. Tall and willowy, she made a seductive figure in a diaphanous silk chiffon robe worn over matching wide-legged trousers. The robe was wisteria-mauve, trimmed with marabou. Behind her came the French brunettes, wearing identical outfits: one almond-blossom, the other pale blue. A murmur of appreciation ran around the crowd. A dapper Chinese switched from snapping the Great Rose Window and instead began to snap the three girls.

Other tourists followed suit. Even the man peddling
souvenirs at the cathedral end of the square
paused mid-sale to take note. A member of
André's corps unlinked the rope and led the girls
into the arena. The crowd swelled.

'Zere.' André indicated a narrow knee-high
stone wall. 'You stand zere.'

'On it?' Neille asked in dismay, for her shoes
were marabou trimmed mules, inappropriate for
rock climbing.

'On it.'

A helper lent a hand and above the ground she
teetered, while the photographer directed his
attention to the other models.

Feeling the warmth of the sun on the back of
her neck, Neille sent up a silent thank you for
small mercies. Goosebumps never photographed
well, but after a chilly start to the final season of
the year the weather had skipped capriciously back
a notch to provide an Indian summer. Another
mercy was that the outfits organised for today did
not—so far as she could ascertain—appear to be
too sheer. Mutely Neille urged André to hurry.
This pose could not be held for long. Not that she
was posing, more standing like a prune on a knife
edge, trusting to luck she would not fall.

She took care to keep her gaze well above the
heads of the crowd. A single day in France had
taught her how every male between six and a
hundred-and-six believed it his bounden duty to
catch your eye, but exchanging steamy glances
with strangers was not her style. What *was* her
style, she wondered? Neille did not know any
more. At the start of her love affair with Simon
she had been carefree and passionate. With Lewis

she was reticent. With Jack—she nearly overbalanced. Jack was a special case, transitory and spurious. He was a 'here today and gone tomorrow' man. She steadied herself. That sly whistling of 'Nellie the Elephant' had been a red-rag challenge. Yesterday's uncertainty had vanished. Neille was on the attack. Now she knew exactly how to spike Mr Rea's guns.

'Arms out,' ordered André, flapping his around as though guiding Concorde into a safe bay.

Gingerly Neille stretched out her arms. Below, on solid ground, the French models spread out their arms, too. A command from André, and six corps members appeared, each with a small bundle cupped in his hands. Two went to each brunette, two came to Neille, climbing awkwardly on to the wall either side of her.

'Good grief!' she gasped, when they shed their cargo. A plump grey pigeon now stood on each outstretched arm.

Her skin crawled. She was not enamoured of birds at the best of times and to have clawed feet tightening and slackening, tightening and slackening, just inches away from her face, made Neille feel slightly sick. Whether the pigeons were drugged, had had their wings clipped, or simply derived a kick from standing on what had become petrified flesh, she did not know, but they made no attempt to fly away. If only they had. After a minute's more shuffling they sat, warm and feathery and horrible, and began to croon. Actually croon!

'You all right, sunbeam?'

'I don't know.' Terrified to move her head, Neille swivelled her eyes to right and left, but could not find Jack. The Chinese man continued to take snapshots and André was yelling at one of the brunettes who was threatening to have hysterics, but no Jack. 'Where are you?' she hissed from the corner of her mouth.

'Behind, to the side. Out of camera, but near enough to catch if you fall.'

'Promise?' she quaked.

'Promise.'

Jack's company had been the last thing she wanted—as Neille had insisted all through breakfast—but now she was grateful. His support wasn't *vital*, of course, but she admitted there was reassurance in having him near. The photographer took his place at the tripod and gave orders, and she managed to raise her head to stare haughtily into the sky. Click went the camera.

'*Profile à gauche,*' commanded André.

Neck sinews moving like rusty steel rods, she inched her head around, giving an involuntary shudder when she discovered the left arm pigeon regarding her from close unblinking range. The other pigeon had begun to fidget.

'Hold on in there, sunbeam.'

'Smile,' commanded André.

She smiled. Inches away the pigeon refused to respond. The camera clicked again. Next Neille was instructed to look right. In tortured slow motion, she obeyed. The right arm pigeon had discovered something among its feathers. A flea? If her arms didn't drop off with exhaustion, if she didn't plummet from the wall in a tailspin, was she then destined to contract some rare ornithological disease? Let it end, she prayed. Let it end. If only that pigeon would stop ferreting around. Then she saw Jack, just a glimpse of his dark head beyond the flea-ridden bird, and felt a totally inappropriate rush of relief, affection almost. He was nodding encouragement and mouthing, 'You're doing fine.' Was she? Really?

'Smile,' urged André. 'Chin higher. Oop, oop, *chérie.*'

Everything ended in confusion. After taking a rapid series of shots, the photographer grinned. *'Merveilleux!'* he cried with uncharacteristic satisfaction, and clapped his hands. At the noise the pigeons took fright. They pinned her arms with needle claws and, in reflex, Neille jerked. The birds took off to soar, she joggled back and forth, and was capsizing when strong arms plucked her from the wall.

'Oh, Jack,' she whimpered, held close and safe against a solid chest. 'Oh, Jack, thank you, thank you.' She nestled her head into the hollow of his shoulder. 'Oh, Jack. You're a lovely man.'

He grinned down. 'I bet you say that to all the guys.'

'I don't!' Neille objected, then saw he was tongue in cheek. 'No, I don't,' she repeated, smiling now.

He *was* lovely. She knew exactly what Dee and the brunettes saw in him. He had lovely grey eyes with lovely thick black lashes. His straight nose was lovely, too. And his mouth, especially his mouth. Why had she never taken time off to study it before? He had full lips with an impudent little crease at each corner. Lost in his nearness, she decided he was the loveliest man she had ever seen. Not as film-star handsome as Simon who, with his silver-blond hair and green eyes, had only needed to take one step into a room to set female eyes popping out on stalks, but more solidly attractive. Jack wasn't a pretty boy, he was a man who had been and seen and done, and his character was etched in his face. Such a lovely face. Neille's hand slid up to curl around the back of his neck where the dark hair waved thickly, and applied pressure. As his head came down, so she reached up and kissed him.

'Hey,' Jack murmured, the creases at the corners of his mouth deepening. 'Hey, what's all this about?'

A second time her hand applied pressure and a second time she kissed him, but this time his lips parted fractionally ahead of hers and the kiss was transferred into a heart-racing, mind-banging, firework-popping, jazz-band-playing extravaganza. If Neille had been in danger of collapsing in a heap after playing hostess to the pigeons, now she was in graver danger of collapsing after playing hostess to the lusty Mr Rea. She may have initiated the embrace, but he had weighed in with his two pennyworth. She felt weak and breathless, and all of a sudden at cross purposes. Had she kissed him by instinct or design? Neille swooped on design. It had to be. Wasn't that her plan? Hadn't she decided that the best way to forestall his threat of moving in was to move in emphatically herself first?

Yet she had never foreseen such a deep degree of personal involvement. Could she carry through her scheme and emerge unscathed? After a kiss like that, there had to be doubts. Neille stiffened her resolve. She must not be faint-hearted. Her breathlessness was simply on account of her not having been kissed properly for ages, nothing else.

The next time she would ensure there was far less spontaneity, and much more deliberation and cool control.

Jack's response had also been spontaneous, but the moment he realised she had been making a pass, that she actively *wanted* them to be glued together, he would gallop off shrieking for solvent. Lewis might have agreed to closer surveillance, but only within understood and confined limits. All she needed to do was pretend to batter down those limits, and Jack would retreat. Integrity mattered to him. She had seen enough of his business dealings to know he was honest, fair and true. Didn't he telephone Lewis and write regular reports? Didn't he keep a close eye on expenses? The man was a professional right down to his fingertips. He might tease and taunt, but that was all. Aware of occupying a positon of trust, Jack would never do anything to put it in jeopardy. Yes, if she pushed he would retreat. Wasn't he retreating now?—firmly unwinding her arms from around his neck and standing back.

'I'm driven to contemplating what that was in aid of,' he said, eyeing her with more than a tinge of circumspection. 'Could it be I'm playing your straight man, yet again?'

'Thank you very much!' Neille chose to present herself as flip. 'I show my appreciation for being rescued and you promptly accuse me of double dealing. You just brim with Old World gallantry, don't you?'

'Sunbeam, when you get me in a clinch before a cast of thousands, it's suspicion I brim with.'

For the first time since he'd rescued her from the wall, Neille became aware of onlookers. André

and the brunettes drew eyes, but she and Jack were
receiving more than their fair share of interested
glances. Appearing in public places in her
professional capacity was something she had
learned to live with, but providing a sideshow was
a different matter.

'I must change,' she announced, and ran across
the square and into the caravan in a flurry of silk
chiffon.

The next tableau featured the brunettes perched
on the wall while Neille had both feet firmly
planted on the paving stones below. No pigeons,
but this time a brown leather boxing glove was
fitted to each fist. The gloves complemented boxer
shorts worn beneath plunge-neck lounge coats.
Neille was in bronze, the other girls in lemon and
chartreuse.

Two hours and four changes of outfit later,
André gave orders that the caravan was to roll.
Jack sweet-talked himself a lift, and they set off for
the Palais de Chaillot. Here their base was a wide
terrace with golden statues, which overlooked
formal gardens spreading down to the Seine.
Beyond the river stood the metal bulk of the Eiffel
Tower, and if you stretched your eyes further you
could see the trees in the Champ de Mars, one of
Paris's best-loved open spaces. Such grand-scale
harmony of design made the terrace a favourite
sight-seeing spot, though once again the tourists
who gathered there were happy to transfer their
interest. The Chinese man appeared—or could this
be a different individual?—and worked his way
through a roll of film.

André shot three different sequences and began
to arrange another. His helpers ran around,

tourists arrived and departed, and late lunch came in the form of spasmodic bites at salad-filled *baguettes*.

'Why not have a proper meal at that café over there?' Neille suggested, as Jack wolfed down a morsel she had smuggled out from the caravan. She had had to smuggle it, because the *baguettes* were supposed to be restricted to official personnel only. 'You could also take time off to ring your office.'

'No need. I called my secretary at home before breakfast and received an update on the current scene. I'm happy to report that, despite my absence, Rea Safeguards is ticking over nicely.'

'And I can also tick over nicely, despite your absence. Go and have lunch. I'm perfectly safe, haven't seen a bazooka or a flick knife in ages, and I won't run away. Honest.'

'You said that once before,' he reminded her, grinning at the grave face which was at odds with her appearance.

Dressed in a style André had christened 'Zee 'Ollywood Cabaret', Neille was resplendent in a tight white basque. The addition of a black top hat tipped at a rakish angle over her copper-gold tresses, a bow tie, cane and high-heeled shoes, had brought whistles from the crowd. In anyone's book she was a stunner, but right now she was too engrossed in ensuring Jack was fed to bother about any effect she might be having.

'I mean it this time,' she assured him, sombre as a witness swearing to tell the truth, the whole truth and nothing but the truth. 'Your Métro madness has changed everything. Do you think I'd risk you leaping into action like that a second time? I give you my solemn word that I'll keep to heel.'

'Funnily enough, I believe you.'

'Good.' Neille stood smiling up at him, then remembered that, although there would be no more escape attempts, she and Jack remained antagonists. Her protests had been channelled into one direction, that was all—coming on strong, *too* strong. And wasn't it time he had a second dose of his medicine? Still smiling, she raised a hand and slowly pushed the incorrigible strand of dark hair back from his brow. She had intended the gesture to appear familiar, tender and flirtatious, all at the same time, but suddenly her nerve failed her. Was she acting or was this for real? Hurriedly she withdrew her fingers before they did something ridiculous, like trembling or smoothing his cheek. 'Now, please vamoose and get yourself a decent meal,' she instructed briskly.

'What, and leave you naked and defenceless?' asked Jack, showing a remarkable capacity for copycat tactics. Her breasts were curving saucily, pushed into smooth firm globes by the boned white satin, and his eyes began to roam over them in a way which contrived to be familiar, tender and flirtatious all rolled into one. Beneath his gaze, Neille's breath seemed to stop, yet her heart was racing. 'Just a figure of speech,' he murmured. 'My God, if Brian could see you now.'

'Brian?' she asked, bemused. This attempt to make Jack uncomfortable had gone disastrously wrong. She had fallen into her own trap.

'Detective Inspector Brian Gilchrist. He was involved in the business of Lewis's nasty letter, so we meet up from time to time.'

FREE BOOKS CERTIFICATE

Dear Susan,

Your special Introductory Offer of 2 Free books is too good to miss. I understand they are mine to keep with the Free Tote Bag.

Please also reserve a Reader Service Subscription for me. If I decide to subscribe I shall receive 4 new books every two months for £4.40 post and packing free. If I decide not to subscribe, I shall write to you within 10 days. The free books will be mine to keep, in any case.

I understand that I may cancel my Subscription at any time simply by writing to you. I am over 18 years of age.

7A6B

Name _____ Signature _____
(BLOCK CAPITALS PLEASE)

Address _____

_____ Postcode _____

Mills & Boon reserve the right to exercise discretion in granting membership. Offer expires 31st December 1986. You may be mailed with other offers as a result of this application. Valid in UK only, overseas please send for details.
Please note Readers in South Africa write to: Independent Book Services P.T.Y., Postbag X3010, Randburg, 2125 South Africa.

NO
STAMP
NEEDED

To Susan Welland
Mills & Boon Reader Service
FREE POST
P.O. Box 236
CROYDON
Surrey CR9 9EL

SEND NO MONEY NOW

'Oh.' That was all Neille could think of to say. Good grief, it wasn't like her to be tongue-tied. She ran back a few steps mentally, and started again. 'This Brian,' she said, leaning on her cane and determinedly throwing out one hip, 'would he think I looked . . . appealing?'

'The *crème de la crème*,' Jack said cheerfully.

'And you? What do you think?'

'Sunbeam——' He started off jauntily, but somehow lost his way. His eyes clouded, he licked his lower lip, then his eyes began to roam again. 'Sunbeam——' His voice was throaty now. 'Sunbeam, I think you are the——'

'*Vite, vite,*' yelled André. 'Neille, *chérie*, over zere. Zee big smile. Kick zee legs. Twirl zee cane.'

She could have throttled him. What had Jack been about to say? She desperately wanted to know. But the moment had gone, lost for ever. Had he been going to reveal she was the *crème de la crème* for him, too? It was possible. Hadn't his grey eyes softened? Hadn't those lovely little creases appeared at the corners of his mouth? Hadn't he been on the brink of admitting he found her immensely, overwhelmingly appealing? Neille released a breath. Who was she fooling? All she represented to Jack Rea was money, a step up the ladder for his damned company. And all he represented to her was a month of irritation, a month which was rapidly coming to an end. Next week Jack would be long gone.

Mid-afternoon they moved camp for the third and final time. Montmartre, renowned as the haunt of painters, musicians and writers, was their destination. Still in essence a hill-top village, Montmartre has a dilapidated charm which acts

like a magnet for tourists. The caravan was parked
in the old Place du Tertre, the hub of activity, and
when Neille peeped out she saw that the cobbled
square was thronged. Degas, Modigliani and
Toulouse-Lautrec had once gathered here, but
now their places had been taken by artists of many
different persuasions. Palette knives wielded acryl-
ics; fingers smeared on oils; charcoal and
watercolours abounded. Silhouettes were being
fashioned from ebony card, and likenesses re-
produced—to varying degrees—in pastels. Some
artists demonstrated more skill at bargaining a
price than in painting a picture, but the crowds
who surrounded the easels did not seem to care.

When Neille and the brunettes made an
entrance, there were cries of 'Bravo' and a round
of applause. Space had been cleared around a
demonstrably French painter with a bushy black
beard and beret, and as they made their way
towards him the press of spectators miraculously
multiplied. It was all the helpers could do to hold
back the crowd.

'Neille, you alone for zees shot. Zee other girls
no boobs. Like so,' ordered André, bending at the
waist to peer into the artist's easel. 'Zee legs apart,
zee *derrière* oop.'

She complied, positioning herself in a manner
which sparked off a second round of applause. She
was not surprised. Clad in a scarlet back-lacing
corset, with bowed suspenders and black seamed
stockings, Neille was uncomfortably aware of
being an out-and-out sex object. By looking up she
could see Jack, mere feet away in the crowd,
grinning. By looking down she could see her
bosom, regrettably on the point of popping out.

One deep breath and she'd be in trouble. Jack might be treating her predicament lightly, but for her the vibes were all wrong. There was too much muttering, too many elbows being nudged, too many beady eyes. Modelling always included an element of sexuality, but the proportions had gone haywire. No matter how André angled his camera, was anyone going to bother about the underwear? Or, like the men in the crowd, were they only going to see pouting round breasts and a vulnerable backside?

Too vulnerable. Suddenly a hand touched her, a hot clammy hand. With a yelp of protest Neille turned, but in one spring Jack was with her, thrusting both the hand and its owner away.

'No, no,' he chided, and she straightened to see him waggling a finger at a surly youth dressed in the leathers of a motor cyclist. The youth's face reddened and he squared up. Was there going to be a fight? Should the *gendarmes* be summoned? The crowd held its collective breath, visualising flying fists, cut lips, bruises, spilled blood. 'Not for you,' Jack said, and winked. He gave her thigh a playful tweak which made her jump. 'For me.'

The square exploded into one enormous guffaw. Everyone was laughing, the youth, André, the brunettes, the helpers, the crowd and—although it took a minute to come to terms—Neille. What could have been a nasty incident had been turned into fun and games. But Jack *had* pinched her bottom. Shouldn't she reciprocate? Wasn't this the perfect time and place to make another, supremely public, pass?

'My knight in blue jeans,' she said, smiling as she placed one hand at his waist, the other on his

shoulder. Neille felt him go very still. 'What would
I do without you?' she enquired, and dabbed a kiss
on his mouth.

Jack did not respond. His grey eyes were
watchful. What happens next? she could hear him
thinking. He had accepted the kisses at Notre
Dame and later her flirting, but now he was
cautious. He might not be exactly running for
cover, but he was definitely reassembling his
thoughts. Neille grinned. She had him at her
mercy. Edging her hand along his belt to his spine,
she then slid it smartly down and deposited two
pert patronising pats on his backside.

'Hey!' he protested, as the crowd roared. 'What
the——?' All set to take her to task, he realised
they were the centre of attention and changed his
mind. Shrugging good-naturedly, he turned to the
photographer. 'OK, André, the floor show's over.
Get cracking.'

The camera session resumed, but this time with
totally different vibes. Established as a woman
with on-call protection, plus a healthy sense of
humour, Neille was no longer up for grabs.
Camaraderie and respect replaced the heavy
breathing, and she was much happier. Her
happiness increased when she realised Jack had
become distracted, not at all his usual self. This
was a morale booster, and although André kept
up the pressure until darkness fell and the
temperature zeroed alarmingly, she never
grumbled. The brunettes might complain about
the cold, but a glow of satisfaction at having
outmanoeuvred Jack kept Neille warm.

Yet getting back into proper clothes was still a
relief. Dressed in sweater, white slacks and parka

once more, she emerged on to the Place du Tertre. The hour and the decrease in temperature had resulted in a general exodus from the square, and the few tourists who remained were far more interested in the canvases exhibited in the lamplight than in a respectably clad girl with an unmade-up face. Only Jack, waiting patiently outside the caravan, looked up as she appeared.

'We must talk,' he said, making no pretence at a greeting. His stance was stiff, his eyes wary. Was he afraid she might thrust out a hand and give him another quick pat?

'What about?' Neille asked, finding it hard not to smile.

'You know what about.'

'Do I?' She looked around. Interspersed with art shops and quaint old cottages, the square contained some interesting restaurants where menus were posted up outside. 'How about us eating in Montmartre tonight?' she suggested. 'It would make a change from the hotel.'

'Suits me, but——'

'Fine. Shall we try here?' Neille tripped over to the nearest eating place, a doll's house with white walls and green painted window shutters. She inspected the menu. 'Good selection,' she appraised, then swished her arm a joyful hundred and eighty degrees. 'Or we could try there, or there, or there.'

'This one, but later.' Jack was unimpressed by her merriment. 'First we'll have a drink *and a talk*.' He stabbed a finger at a nearby inn. 'Let's go,' he commanded, using a voice guaranteed to inspire rapid obedience.

Shabby, in a comfortable lived-in kind of way,

the inn had old horse brasses and faded paintings covering whitewashed walls. They found a table in a quiet corner, and Neille waited as he fetched a carafe of dry white wine.

'Cheers,' she smiled, raising her glass. 'I'd like to thank you for pinching my bottom. Very cleverly you rescued me and defused the situation, all in one. I never thought I'd admit freely to this, but it felt good having you around.'

'Nice to know I have my uses,' he said cryptically.

Neille placed an elbow on the table which sat between them, resting her chin on her hand. 'Want to pinch me again?' she enquired.

'And have you demanding a return bout? No, thank you.'

'Now, Jack,' she grinned. 'You're coming on like you're untouched by human hand.'

'I'm coming on like I have a sense of responsibility towards my employer, who happens to be Lewis Mitchell, *your* boyfriend. He's paying for me to be here with you, and us——' He flung her a violent glare. '—and us messing around is dishonourable.'

Neille twisted a strand of coppery hair around her finger. 'I understood Lewis had given his permission for us to . . . mess around? *Carte blanche*, you said. We could be lovers, courtesy of Lewis, you said. And maybe I'll discover I like it, you said.' Her grin was impish. 'Guess what—I have!'

'Quit acting,' he ordered grittily.

Her wholesome *ingénue* smile was trotted out. 'Who's acting?'

'You are. You know damned well that I said all that just as a device to try and make you behave.'

Her eyes seemed to grow to twice their size.
'Lewis didn't agree you could . . . move in?'

'Yes, he did,' Jack snapped. 'But on a purely
businesslike footing.'

'How can lovers be businesslike?' she enquired
with mock naïveté.

'Cut it out, Neille. I got carried away and
painted the picture up a bit, that's all,' he growled.
'Dammit, I never intended to *do* anything. It was
to be looks, words, innuendoes. I wanted to keep
you guessing, wondering if. OK, it's not in the rule
book, but then neither are you!' Exasperation had
raised his voice, and he needed to make a
conscious effort to lower it. 'Usually my charges
co-operate,' he hissed. 'They ask my advice on
what to do for the best, and when I make
suggestions they follow them, to the letter. They
most certainly don't insult me sixteen hours a day,
nor leave me to rot outside public lavatories,
nor——'

'Call you Jackson?'

'Damned right,' he glowered.

'How about patting your bottom?' Her eyes
sparkled. 'You have such a sexy bottom.'

His jaw clenched. 'Don't push it, Neille.'

'As if I would. You were very quick on the draw
where the motor cyclist was concerned. Most
impressive,' she continued. 'Now I understand
how you've gained such a fine reputation.'

'And now I understand you're buttering me up.
But the motor cyclist was no threat.'

'He could have been my assassin.'

Jack shook his head. 'There isn't an assassin.'

'You don't know that.'

He poured out second helpings of wine. 'As this

appears to be true confessions time, I'll carry on. From the start you've insisted no one's gunning, and I may as well admit I agree.'

'But you've always maintained there was a risk,' she protested.

'There is, one which equates with being nibbled to death by a crazed hamster.'

'You said it was common sense to be on the alert,' Neille rebuked. 'On the alert for a crazed hamster?'

'I needed to justify my existence, didn't I?' he thrust back. 'I've told Lewis on numerous occasions that I consider myself superfluous, but he refuses to listen. He says he's booked me for a month, so a month it'll stay. *I* recognise I'm taking money under false pretences, but if I'd let that slip you'd have made mincemeat out of me.'

'I did think you operated in a funny way,' she confessed. 'Letting me carry on my everyday life when I was supposed to be being tracked by a killer.'

Jack drank some wine. 'Well, now you know. Even the police've advised Lewis not to take the matter to heart. Their theory, and I agree, is that putting threats down on paper was enough to satisfy whoever wrote the note. If someone really means business they make sure they're specific, not woolly. That note was beginning and end.'

'Do the police have any idea where the photograph of Lewis and me fits in?'

'Sorry, there are no theories on that score.' He threw her a glance. 'You've never jilted a guy, have you? Given someone cause to take offence? People can seek vengeance in some strange and nasty ways.'

'No,' she said, as a cold finger of fear touched her spine. Jack was referring to the past, but might he not equally be talking about the future? 'No,' Neille repeated, frightened to dwell on what might happen if the lingerie photographs did not have the required effect. 'I met Simon when I was seventeen and was faithful to him until he died.' A sadness welled in her eyes, then she shrugged and it was gone. 'Since then, apart from the occasional casual outing, I've dated Lewis.' She drained her glass. 'Shall we go and eat?'

The doll's house frontage was misleading. Once inside, the building opened out into an assortment of dining rooms linked by stone--flagged corridors.

'S'il vous plaît,' said a waiter, leading them off on what seemed a mile-long trek past kitchens and stores, stillrooms and offices. But the journey proved worthwhile, for he finally brought them to a bijou dining room where flickering candles provided a golden light, and a violinist was playing a love song. Dark blue velvet covered the tables, there was a posy of violets, and each menu was adorned with cherubs. 'Romantic, eh?' smiled the waiter.

Neille grinned at Jack. 'Soft lights, sweet music and a hefty helping of steamed rabbit, who could ask for more?'

He obliged with a theatrical groan.

The meal passed in the same light-hearted mood. They appeared to have taken a step forward and could now be friends. With a pang, Neille recognised that their relationship could have been like this from the start, if she had co-operated. But time was running out.

'Can you rustle up your coat while I settle the bill?' Jack enquired, finishing his liqueur.

'Will do.'

Earlier her parka had been whisked away, and now the waiter who knew its exact whereabouts had become involved in serving a table of ten. Rather than hang around, Neille decided to go in search herself. A wooden sign indicated the cloakrooms, and as Jack headed for the cashier's desk by the front door, she set off in the direction of the arrow. She passed two unmarked doors and came out into a square lobby. Which way now? A second sign indicated right. Right meant another long corridor, and she was making her way down it when she became aware of footsteps clip-clopping along behind. Someone else was obviously tracking down their coat, too. Neille was tempted to stop and commiserate, but the realisation that the person behind might well not speak English kept her silent. The corridor ended in a T-junction. She looked both ways. There was a faded sign further along the wall to the left. Could that indicate cloakrooms?

When she had stopped, so the steps behind had stopped, and now, as she started to walk again, so the footsteps started. How the eeriness occurred, Neille did not know. It appeared, not by degrees, but precipitately and frighteningly. She was being stalked. Since leaving the dining room there had been no signs of life, no voices, and she was aware of being marooned in a maze with a stranger. No, she was being over-sensitive. All she needed to do was turn and grin, then everything would be fine. But there was no chance to turn and grin because suddenly a hand brushed her shoulder, she felt fingers touch her hair. From behind came a soft chuckle, a soft, pleased, male chuckle. Fear hurtled her forward, but her acceleration was braked as the hand tightened, forcing back her head.

The surly youth had returned! He might have joined in the laughter this afternoon, but now he had tracked her down. He would want revenge, and that meant far more than just touching her this time. Trapped by her hair, Neille could not escape, but even so a fearful paralysis had rooted her to the spot.

'No. Please, no.'

Did she say the words out loud? The hand, once again hot and clammy, moved to caress her neck, and she squeaked in alarm—an ineffectual squeak. But standing and squeaking was the action of a mouse. She wasn't a mouse. Hadn't her years growing up with Peter, Paul and Podge ensured she possessed no hang-ups about women being useless, frail creatures? Hadn't they praised her, if grudgingly, because she could always be relied upon to fight? Why not fight now? She took a deep breath, raised her arm, clenched her fist. Wham! Neille hit the man behind her a fierce blow on the cheek.

'Oh!' If she had hit the seven-headed Beast of the Apocalypse, she would not have been more surprised for, instead of hitting the youth in leathers, as expected, she had hit a Chinese man in a navy blue suit. 'Oh!' she said again.

He was leaning against the wall, a hand to his cheek. Then, to her astonishment, he smiled. 'Pretty girl, Neille,' he said. 'Pretty girl.'

She couldn't believe it. She had walloped him

and there he stood, chanting, 'Pretty girl, Neille. Pretty girl.' He reminded her of an evil parrot, ready to swoop and peck out her eyes. In terror and confusion, she pushed past and charged headlong down the passage, instinctively heading for sound. There were no footsteps behind her now. Face scarlet, breath coming in laboured gasps, Neille burst into the front hall. Jack was talking to the lady cashier, while nearby stood the waiter, holding her parka.

'Thanks.' She plucked it from him and ran, bundling Jack with her out on to the street in an impassioned rush. 'Jack, oh Jack,' she jabbered, clutching hold of his arm. 'Jack, there's a man in there. A man—a man——' Her chest rose and fell, but fear clogged her throat and she could not say the words. 'Oh, Jack. Thank goodness you're here,' she blabbed, and collapsed against him.

'Cut it out, Neille,' he ordered. 'You've pulled this stunt once too often. I thought we'd agreed that us ... messing around was out of the question.'

She gazed at him, wide-eyed. 'What?'

'I'm not going to kiss you,' he said, holding his arms stiffly by his sides. 'Even if you don't feel you owe Lewis any loyalty, I do. Now, put on your coat and——'

'Jack, there's a man in there who——' As she flung on her parka, her voice started squeaking again. 'Who—who touched me.'

'Good for him, but I'm not going to.'

'Jack, listen!'

'No, *you* listen. I'm not going to touch you, or hold you close, or ... anything! So you can stop this act.' As he spoke, he had begun backing away down the pavement. Neille followed. 'OK, I find you attractive, very attractive. And I admit I kissed you this morning, but that was a mistake. You took me by surprise when you fell off the wall. But it won't happen twice, Neille. This time I have my priorities well and truly sorted out. I don't want to kiss you again. In other circumstances—well, there aren't any other circumstances, are there? If there were maybe it'd be different, but it's not.' He ran a hand through his hair. 'Am I making sense? Maybe I do want to kiss you. Yes, I do. Very much. In fact, if you really want to know, I'd like nothing better than to get you into bed right now, but I'm not going to because I happen to believe in the sanctity of the employer/employee relationship. Lewis is paying me, which means I don't cheat on the guy. And don't look at me like that. It doesn't matter that you're the most desirable woman I've met in years; what matters is that I refuse to tarnish a reputation which I've worked damned hard to build up over——'

'Jack!' Neille tugged at his sleeve. 'Jack, you don't understand. I've met the assassin.'

CHAPTER SIX

'THE who?'

'The assassin, the villain, the man who sent Lewis his note.'

Jack halted in his retreat. 'What the hell are you talking about?'

'The man who touched me.' Her fingers tightened on his sleeve. She was desperate for contact. Jack was big and male and protective, and she needed him. 'He knew my name. When I hit him he said, "Pretty girl, Neille".' She shuddered at the memory. 'It was weird. Perhaps he's paranoid or schizophrenic or——'

'You hit a guy?' he interrupted.

'Yes, yes.' Neille bobbed her head up and down. 'He followed me along the corridor and when I stopped, he stopped. Then he put out his hand and touched my hair. I thought it must be the motor cyclist who'd groped me this afternoon but it wasn't and—and I hit him.'

Jack was looking at her as if she was stark staring mad. 'You hit a complete stranger just because he touched your hair?'

'Yes, and I hurt him,' Neille said, with a burst of pride. It was a pity her cousins hadn't been there. They would have admired her fighting style. 'When he staggered back, there was a big red mark on his cheek.' She put both hands on Jack's arm and pulled. 'Come along, we must go and find him before he has a chance to get

away. You can make a citizen's arrest or
something.'

'Hang on.' Jack placed his hand over the two
which were attempting to drag him towards the
restaurant and held them still. 'Would you please
tell me exactly what's happened?'

'But there's no time to lose,' she cried, putting
on pressure. 'The man might escape. I'll fill you in
on the details later. *Come on*.'

He stood firm. 'No way. You're not getting me
back in there. In fact, our best bet is to exit
Montmartre, and fast. The police may well be
arriving at any minute. It's not a bodyguard you
need, it's a bloody straitjacket. You can't go around
slugging innocent bystanders for no reason at all.'

'Innocent? No reason? He touched me!'

'The guy was admiring your hair. It's an
unusual colour and——'

'No, Jack. He grabbed hold and jerked back
my head,' she insisted feverishly. 'I couldn't get
free.'

'Isn't it more likely you stumbled and he
reached out to save you?' He held up a hand to
silence the protests which were bubbling from her
lips and listened. 'Wasn't that a police siren?'

'I didn't hear anything, but if it was—great!
When they arrive we can tell them everything. How
he followed me down the corridor, how he——'

'*We* tell them? No thanks, if you don't mind I'll
sit this one out,' Jack said, and began prising her
fingers from his sleeve.

'You don't believe I did come face to face with
the assassin, do you?' she demanded, snatching her
hand away.

He moved his shoulders. 'Assassin? Frankly,

no.' When he saw how she scowled, he added, 'So sue me.'

'What a very good idea,' Neille flared. 'I was under the impression you were responsible for my safety, but am I safe? Am I hell! While you were having a great time, flashing credit cards and chatting up that cashier, I could have been raped and murdered. Or kidnapped. Yesterday you bugged me, today you didn't bother. I could have ended up bound and gagged in a car heading for Monte Carlo, and no one would've been any wiser.' Her tirade ceased without warning. 'Do you really want to go to bed with me?'

'Very much so.' Jack tilted his head. 'And that *was* a siren, so move it. If I let you get arrested by the French police, Lewis'll never forgive me.'

Employing brute force in preference to friendly persuasion, he grabbed hold of her hand and began propelling her from the Place du Tertre. Down a narrow cobbled street they went, him striding while Neille skittered alongside in her high-heeled boots. The street plunged sharply downhill and keeping pace on a steep incline was no easy task. Below them spread Paris, the lights twinkling like diamonds in the black velvet distance.

'What did this assassin of yours look like?' Jack enquired, easing up when several hundred yards had been put between them and the restaurant.

Neille frowned, attempting to assemble an Identikit picture. 'Short, skinny, with sleek black hair. A typical Chinese.'

He stopped in his tracks. 'The guy was Chinese?'

She nodded. 'Around forty, though it's hard to tell.'

'Don't say any more, let me guess,' he ordered, a

chuckle beginning to rumble. 'He was wearing a long crimson robe and one of those little black caps? With a pigtail down his back? And he said——' Jack demonstrated a low bow. 'Ah so, Missie Neille, you have velly plitty hair?' The chuckle had grown into a belly laugh, and it was fortunate they had stopped beside a street lamp because now he needed to hold on to remain upright. 'Chinese?' he gasped. 'You were locked in mortal combat with a refugee from a Hong Kong triad? Neille, you're a killer!'

'So mock,' Neille snapped, refusing to admit to any doubts. She powered off downhill alone.

'You must see the funny side,' he said, catching up. 'As an assassin, the guy sounds a great Sunday School teacher.'

She marched on. 'He grabbed hold of my hair and touched my neck. His hand felt horrible and— and I was *frightened*,' she wailed. Neille had never intended to wail, indeed she had been grinding out her tale from between gritted teeth, but something inside her crumpled. She was weary of being the fighter, of giving as good as she got. Peter, Paul and Podge might well hoot with scorn, but all she wanted was to be pampered.

'I'm sorry.' Jack's voice was low. He slid an arm around her shoulders and drew her to a halt. 'Forgive me?' He brushed a tendril of hair from her cheek. 'I shouldn't have laughed. Whatever happened, it can't have been pleasant.'

'It wasn't.' Her words emerged on a sob.

'You're trembling.' He pulled her into his arms and began patting her back, comforting her. 'Oh sunbeam, don't. You're safe. I'm here. I'll look after you.'

'Even Nellie the Elephant gets scared sometimes,' she gulped, trying hard to smile. But his concern had lowered her resistance and Neille, who rarely cried, felt a tear run down her cheek.

'Sunbeam,' Jack said brokenly, and began smoothing her hair, touching her face with his fingers, murmuring reassurances.

He bent to kiss the tear away and then, somehow, his mouth moved lower until it covered hers, soft and warm and comforting. When and where the comfort stopped and the desire began was never entirely clear, but as Neille's arms slid up around his neck, so Jack's lips coaxed hers apart. Instinctively she nestled against him, drawing strength from his mouth and deep, deep pleasure. Heat began to glow, running along her limbs, radiating through her body, and with the heat came an ache, a poignant reminder of how long it was since she had been held close and loved, and how ripe she was for the taking.

'Jack,' she murmured, drawing back.

Did he read the message in her eyes? He must.

'No.' He laid a finger across her lips. 'No,' he repeated gravely and withdrew. Just one short step, but enough to break all contact. He pushed his hands into his trouser pockets and studied his shoes. 'No, the Chinese guy wasn't an assassin.'

Neille gazed at him. How could he be so calm, so rational? He had said he wanted to make love to her, kissed her as though he did, and yet . . . Had passion gripped him as it had gripped her, or had the sweet desire which had flavoured the embrace been purely her imagination?

'My guess is that he's the guy we saw taking

pictures at Notre Dame,' Jack continued, using a neutral voice. 'He must have followed us here. He meant no harm, I'm sure.'

Why this obsession with the assassin? The assassin didn't matter any more. She was beginning to have doubts about the Chinese wanting to hurt her herself. Maybe her accusations had been on the wild side? Maybe she had over-reacted? She wished Jack would let the subject drop. Other matters were far more important. This ache of hers for instance. Couldn't he guess how much she needed him? How much she wanted to——The obvious struck. She had believed his talk of wanting to make love, but it had been empty male swaggering. Akin to men in their late fifties who leered and said, 'My word, I'd be after you if I was twenty years younger.' If. The word was a barricade to hide behind, like Jack had chosen to hide behind Lewis. How very convenient! She had responded to what she had thought was genuine affection and now she was being rejected. But worse things had happened and she had survived.

Neille's chin snapped up. 'It's my guess he followed me over on the plane,' she announced, her stare advising that no one fooled around with her emotions for long, least of all some two-bit bodyguard. 'He was sat next to you.'

Not for one moment did she believe what she had said, but at least it proved she was equally adept at dismissing the embrace.

Jack laughed. 'That guy was Japanese.'

'Japanese. Chinese. They're all oriental.'

'A Japanese who had an onward flight booked to the Far East. I overheard him asking the stewardess if there was a chance he'd still make his connection.'

'Clever clogs!' she snarled, and strode off down the hill again. But as she strode along, her mood began to falter. What was she achieving by acting like a five-year-old? Not much. Why not be more mature? 'OK, I was wrong,' she admitted, throwing him a glance, half apologetic, half rebellious. 'The Chinese man didn't mean me any harm. On second thoughts, maybe I did stumble. My heels are rather high. And as far as knowing my name is concerned, I expect he overheard André giving instructions.'

'I expect he did,' Jack agreed calmly.

Gratitude at him not crowing over her repentance made Neille able to continue. 'Perhaps as a foreigner with poor English all he could say to explain touching my hair was "Pretty girl, Neille".'

'Now you're making sense.'

She looked at him sheepishly. 'I know I've always rejected the notion that someone's out to get me, but——'

'No one is, sunbeam,' he assured her.

'I accept that, but I think maybe in my subconscious there could have been a tiny bit of doubt.'

'Banish it.' Jack was firm. 'Like I said before, Lewis's note fulfilled its purpose by allowing someone to let off steam, and that's an end to it. Believe me?'

Neille nodded. 'I do.'

'That's my girl,' he grinned.

They had reached the bottom of the hill. A taxi was disgorging passengers on a corner and Jack steered her towards it. After he'd given the driver the name and location of their hotel, they both climbed in.

'I understood Dee was your girl?' she questioned, as the taxi set off. She flashed a glance through the shadows. 'The two of you always seem to be closeted together, though it beats me what you can find to talk about. I'd have thought five minutes conversation was severely stretching her powers of concentration.'

He gave a wide smile. 'I do love a woman who can disguise her jealousy.'

'Jealous! Me jealous of that cross-eyed little—little—huh!'

'As a matter of fact, we talk about you,' he revealed. 'Dee provides the lowdown on your timetable, and she does a fine job. For example, if you tell me you're due at Knightsbridge at ten-thirty, I check with her. Lo and behold, it has been known to be Chelsea at ten.'

'Trust her to snitch.' Neille huddled closer into the corner of the back seat. Not only did Jack spurn, now he was admitting to underhand tricks with a sly confederate.

'Dee's been a good friend,' he protested.

'Lucky you.' Was she jealous? How could anyone be jealous of Dee? The girl was a colourless individual, though pretty enough in a milkmaid kind of a way. He didn't really like her, did he? Jack needed someone who would meet him as an equal, not an inane yes-woman. 'What was your wife like?' she found herself asking.

He gave a surprised grunt. 'Five foot four, fair hair, brown eyes.'

'No, I mean as a person.'

'Friendly, articulate, a go-getter.'

'That doesn't sound such a bad combination.'
She sat up straighter. 'Why the divorce?'

'Why the sudden interest?' he countered.

Neille shrugged. 'You've compiled a dossier on
me. Isn't it time I assembled a few facts about
you? Fair?' she enquired, when he hesitated.

'Fair,' he agreed, after a moment. Jack let out a
breath. 'We divorced because basically I wasn't
prepared to go and get what Kay wanted to go
and get. Or to compromise.'

When he let out a second reflective breath,
indicating that talking about his past wasn't easy
for him, Neille felt sympathetic. Error-strewn
memories were apparently something they had in
common. She gave an encouraging smile.

'Explain, please.'

'I was in the Army at the time and——' He
paused, then set off again at a sturdier rate. 'And
the nature of the job meant I was posted around
different bases in fairly rapid succession. The
constant moving didn't prove conducive to marital
bliss, because Kay was eager to put down roots.
Her idea of "going" was to a stylish Thames-side
village, and her idea of "getting" was a picturesque
cottage in that village. Home-making was a fetish
with her. She had folders full of colour schemes,
room settings. She knew exactly what she wanted,
down to the pattern of the bedroom curtains. The
accommodation the Services provided fell far short
of her requirements. They don't go a bundle on
thatched cottages with mullioned windows,' Jack
said pithily. 'As her dissatisfaction grew, she
started to nag me to buy myself out of the Army.
But I enjoyed the life and I dug in my heels. It was

selfish, but I refused to sit down and talk, to see things from her point of view. My only excuse is that I was young.' He gave a rueful laugh. 'Funnily enough I want now what she wanted then.'

'Mullioned windows?'

He grinned. 'No. Roots, the settled life.'

'A nest?' Neille suggested.

He gave her an odd look. 'That's right. However, our marriage began to disintegrate. When the next posting occurred I moved, but Kay went home to her mother's. The inevitable happened. We were both lost and lonely, and for my part—well.' Jack spread his hands. 'There's something about a uniform which attracts women, and I confess I didn't put up much of a fight to protect my virtue. Then Kay telephoned one day. She'd met someone at a squash club and wanted her freedom. I know it doesn't make sense, but when she said "divorce"—phew! Up to that point I'd managed to persuade myself we were just going through a bad patch, but then I couldn't pretend any more. I had to admit to failing at the single most important relationship in anyone's life. I was shattered. In retaliation I began to sleep around. I suppose I was proving to myself that I wasn't a complete failure with the opposite sex.'

'Did it work?'

'No.' He gave a rueful grin. 'Did you think it would?'

Neille shook her head. 'But it's amazing how adept we all are at deluding ourselves. And how easy it is to analyse our actions, given hindsight.'

'You've discovered that, too?'

'I have. How long was it before you realised the futility of what you were doing?'

'Four, five years.' Jack grunted in self-disgust. 'I'm a slow learner. Since leaving the Army I've had a couple of moderately long-term relationships, but never anything which . . . clicked.'

'Perhaps something'll click with Dee?' she suggested, cloaking what suddenly seemed a turning-point question in casual garb.

'Yeah! There's as much chance of something clicking between her and me as there is of something clicking between Mr Mitchell and you.'

Relief that the secretary meant nothing was swept away by his abrupt insertion of Lewis into the conversation. Dee could be dismissed, Lewis was an entirely different matter. How much had Jack guessed about their relationship?

'And what does that mean?' she enquired, playing for time.

'That, like Dee and me, you and Lewis have nothing in common.' He threw her a look. 'And you can forget about becoming evasive. It took less than seventy-two hours for me to realise you tolerate the man—just. You never ring him, you never mention his name unless you're forced to.' Jack grinned. 'It's being generous to say you're apathetic. However did the two of you get together in the first place?'

'By—by mistake,' Neille admitted, faltering a little. How candid dare she be? There was no point fobbing Jack off with a load of lies, he wouldn't be fooled; yet equally she must not be rash. Criticisms and exposures must be tempered, because right now Lewis remained a potent factor in her life. Allowing herself the dizzy image of the freedom a week Friday might—*would*—bring, was premature.

'You met through your father?' he prompted, when she remained silent.

She nodded. 'Lewis called round one day to deliver some papers. Daddy was out, but I felt it my duty to offer a cup of tea.'

'And he liked what he saw?'

'I'm afraid so. This was two years ago when the "little girl" look was in. I was wearing a dark dress with a big white collar.' Neille's natural spark had her grinning. 'That first impression must have hit him like a sledge hammer, because no matter what I wear now Lewis still regards me as fresh out of a convent. Amazing, isn't it?'

Jack laughed. 'Like you said, we're all adept at deluding ourselves. A convent girl is obviously what Lewis requires.' He sobered. 'Two years ago makes it around the time Simon Gates died?'

'Lewis entered my life just after Simon left it,' she agreed, frowning. She accepted that her questions about Jack's past entitled him to enquire into hers, but suddenly felt threatened. Her head ruled any discussion concerning Lewis, but with Simon her heart would be involved. 'I was very down, very subdued,' she said carefully. 'There was a long period after Simon died when I felt . . . numb. Where I was, what I did, or who I was with scarcely mattered. Lewis and I had the tea, and my father arrived. In his presence Lewis asked if I'd care to join him for dinner. I must confess I was all set to refuse, but—but I saw the look on Daddy's face.'

'He didn't want you to offend the boss?'

'No. I allowed myself to be swayed.' Neille

decided to be pert. She had successfully avoided
talking about Simon and now if she gave him the
facts about Lewis in the form of an anecdote, maybe
he'd treat them as such. Whatever happened, Jack
must not be allowed to pry. 'Dinner proved to be
both painless and expensive. We went to the
Dorchester. Lewis talked about the wonders he was
performing at Mitchells', and I obliged by
contributing the odd murmur. Which suited me fine.'

Jack was watching her closely. 'I presume he
commiserated over Simon's death?'

'Good heavens, no. And thank goodness.' She
gave a peal of laughter. 'I couldn't have borne it if
he had. Lewis was very . . . tactful.'

'You surprise me.' The comment was dry.
'From what I've heard tact isn't one of his
attributes. Could it simply have been he wasn't
interested? Sorry.' He held up a hand. 'Maybe *I'm*
not being tactful.' They had reached the fifth
arrondissement, and Jack leaned forward to direct
the taxi driver. 'So that was the start of a beautiful
friendship?' he said, sitting back. 'I presume?'

'You presume right,' Neille agreed airily.
'Though due to Lewis frequently being away on
business it's a spasmodic friendship. He calls me—
oh, roughly once a fortnight.'

'But you always say yes?'

'Why not?'

Jack gave her a level look. 'Shouldn't it be
"why"? I thought we'd established you and Lewis
aren't exactly on the same wavelength?'

'You might have established it, I haven't,' she
protested, horribly aware of being shuffled into a
corner. 'I agree he's a bit . . . pedestrian, but he's
not all bad.'

'I didn't say he was bad. I just said——'

'We're not lovers,' Neille announced, not quite knowing why.

'I know that. Give me credit for some intelligence.' A tightening of his jaw indicated Jack was running out of patience. 'I'd just like you to explain why you continue to see him. He may be your father's boss, but that doesn't mean you're bound to him with hoops of steel. What the hell does Mitchell have to offer?'

She squirmed. 'You wouldn't understand.'

'Try me.'

'*Eh, bien!*' cried the taxi driver.

They had arrived at the hotel.

Neille knew she had had a close escape. She charged out of the taxi and into the lobby in double quick time. Spouting excuses about needing her sleep quota, she bade him a fast farewell, only to be disconcerted when he agreed he was also ready for bed. In the lift she refused to meet his eyes, terrified a glance might spark off his questions again, but Jack remained silent. A mumbled 'Good night,' in the corridor, and Neille achieved her goal—the solitude of her bedroom. She needed to put space between them, needed time in which to think. Had she revealed too much about her relationship with Lewis, or too little? Jack wouldn't report back, she trusted him on that, so maybe she could have afforded to have thrown more light on the odd coupling? Or maybe not. But leaving Jack dissatisfied could prove unwise.

With a troubled sigh, she began to undress. The clarinettist was well into his evening recital. If he ran true to form he would stop in a few minutes, but for now each note sounded crystal clear. Jack's movements through the wall were also crystal clear. Like her, he was undressing. Neille's movements speeded up. She didn't want to hear him, didn't want her traitorous senses going with him every step of the way. Was his chest hairy? How big was that scar on his shoulder? Did he sleep in the nude? She ripped off her clothes down to her black silk teddy, and sped into the bathroom to embark on a vigorous cleaning of her teeth. While the brush was in action she could not hear him; when she finished she could. His bed springs had twanged. Was he sitting down to remove his shoes, or lying there without a stitch on?

Neille was sorting out her clothes, determinedly paying no attention to the noises from next door, when a movement caught her eye. Hadn't the knob on the door which connected her room with room 41 twitched? Standing still, she waited. Yes, very slowly it was being turned back and forth. Because she had never heard sounds, she had automatically presumed the room to be unoccupied, but someone was in there now. A someone who seemed inordinately interested in the connecting door.

Her first thought was to knock on Jack's wall and demand he come round, but ... He would consider she was panicking again, or maybe jump to the conclusion she was pursuing him on a made up pretext. She would manage without him. The door was locked. It must be. There was no cause for alarm. The knob had stilled, so whoever stood on the other side was not about to burst in. Neille took stock. There seemed no immediate danger, but although she did not fear an assassin it would be difficult to sleep easily without the reassurance that her room was secure. The solution was to indulge in a spot of knob turning herself.

Tiptoeing over, she stretched out cautious fingers and eased the knob anti-clockwise. As the door was hinged to open into her room, she tugged. Nothing happened. Neille had relaxed when, without thinking, she gave a turn and tug in the other direction. The door gave way, swung open. With a gasp of surprise she fell back. Room 41 was in darkness. She could see nothing, no one, but she could smell peppermint.

CHAPTER SEVEN

THE porter must be on the prowl, she reasoned. Neille was peering into the gloom, attempting to discern a shape, when suddenly a hand shot out from room 41, grabbed the knob and slammed shut the door. A lock clicked and then—silence. Looking at the closed door, she gave a startled laugh. What did she do now? Report him, go round to confront him, or what? Maybe it would be wise to tell Jack what had happened? He was the expert and he would know the best action to take.

She stepped out into the corridor and knocked at his door. A glance along to room 41 showed no movement. Presumably the porter was still inside?

'Jack,' she hissed. 'Can I speak to you?'

No reply. Where was he? Surely she would have heard if he'd gone out? 'Jack!' She knocked again. The porter, with his roving eyes, had looked a nasty piece of work and Jack's declaration about 'How can any of us know what a twisted mind will decide?' suddenly echoed. The porter might not have a twisted mind, but he had been cornered and might well retaliate. She did not intend to panic, but all the same she cast a fearful glance at the door of room 41. Was he ready to leap out at any minute? 'Jack!' She pounded a fist. He couldn't be asleep, could he? Her eyes flew back along the corridor. What did the porter intend to do? 'Jack! Please!'

Her fist hit empty air and Neille catapulted

forward, knocking Jack off balance. Instinctively he grabbed hold and took her with him as he buckled at the knees and collapsed back on to the bed.

'Not again,' he groaned, gasping as she lay spread-eagled on top of him. 'What's happened this time? You've found a mass murderer on the window-sill, or has Count Dracula dropped in for a quick bite?'

'No, it's the porter. He's snooping around in room 41. Oh Jack, I had an awful shock. I opened the connecting door and——'

'*You* opened it? Why?'

'Well, the handle turned and—and——' Neille broke off as an overwhelming need for comfort took precedence. Maybe she hadn't been terrified, but she had been a little bit scared. She nestled closer. His skin felt slightly damp. He smelled of soap, clean and male. His chest *was* hairy, covered in whorls of gleaming black hair. She rubbed her cheek against it and when he moved beneath her, she sighed. She was safe now. 'Oh Jack,' she murmured. 'Oh Jack!' The second time it was an exclamation, sharp and surprised. 'You're naked.'

'I thought you'd never notice,' he drawled, as Neille scrambled from him, a whirl of confusion with pink cheeks and tumbled hair.

Where did she look? What did she do? So many times she had seen Simon naked—first in the days when lovemaking had been all, and later when she had taken pity on his stupors and undressed him and put him to bed—but Jack was not Simon. Simon had been as beautiful as an alabaster statue, but never aggressively male. Jack was male. And aggressive. And aroused.

'I presume the porter wasn't naked when you paid him a call?' he asked, reaching for his jeans. He slid into them and stood up. 'I'd better go careful with my zip,' he remarked laconically.

'Yes. No.' Neille, her heart beating like a drum and her breath hard won, was unable to share this controlled amusement. 'No, the porter wasn't naked. Were you under the shower?'

'Just stepped in. I think maybe I'd better get back under and turn it to cold?' he suggested.

'Yes.' She twisted her fingers.

'Would you care to explain what you've been up to this time?' Jack asked, courteous as a duke from days of old.

'Yes.' Neille took a steadying breath. 'As I was getting ready for bed I noticed that someone appeared to be testing the knob on the connecting door,' she said, determined not to ramble. 'When the knob stopped turning, I decided to test it, too. To make certain the door was locked. I turned it one way and—zilch. But when I turned it the other way, the door came open.'

'And the porter was stood there?'

'No,' she confessed, 'but there was a strong smell of peppermints. And then, seconds later, an arm shot out and closed the door.' She glanced to check how she was doing, and saw from his frown that he was taking her seriously. 'As far as I know, no one's come out of room 41 since.'

'I'd better investigate,' Jack said, pulling a sweater on over his head.

'Shall I come, too?'

He grinned, his eyes moving down to remind her how she was wearing her teddy, a flimsy garment cut high on the thigh and low on the bosom.

'You'd better stay here. It'll be kinder on the blood pressure—mine. Keep the door shut and don't open it to anyone but me.'

The tinge of cops and robbers in his instruction proved contagious.

'Shouldn't we have a password?' Neille suggested.

He pushed his feet into his sneakers. 'How about "bodycheck"?'

'What does that mean?'

'It's an ice hockey term which describes one player's deliberate obstruction of another.' The creases at the corners of his mouth deepened. 'A rough assessment of your attitude towards me over the past weeks,' he declared, and was gone.

Neille sat on the bed and waited. She couldn't decide whether she wanted him to trap the porter or not. Proof she hadn't been letting her imagination run away with her would be agreeable, and yet . . . Alarm caused shivers. She remembered the porter's mean eyes. Should she follow in case there was a fight? Competent as Jack was, he had no immunity against a blade between the ribs. Having half risen, she sank down. She must stay put. Stop these disturbing flights of fantasy. Jack had given orders and he was in charge. Five minutes agonised into ten. Why hadn't he come? The porter had looked weedy, he wouldn't be difficult to overpower. But suppose the man in room 41 had not been the porter?

'Bodycheck,' recited a burnt-toast voice.

'What happened? Are you all right? Whatever took you so long?' As she sprang to let him in, so her hands spread themselves across his chest. He was tall and dark, and so very, very lovely that she

was tempted to cry. Having reassured herself there
were no knives sticking out of him, no blood
stains, Neille brought her arms down to her sides.
'Did you find the porter in room 41?' she enquired,
ultra sensible.

'I did, which means I owe you an apology.' Jack
grinned. 'When you burst in and flattened me I
must admit I had reservations, but I was wrong.
Just now, as I left you, I——'

'Just now?' she objected. 'That was centuries
ago.'

His grin widened. 'Centuries ago, as I went
along the corridor, our mint-sucking friend stuck
his head out of room 41, then popped it back in.
Thanks to luck and one massive leap, I managed
to get my foot in the door. After a spell of me
push-you push, he decided to give in gracefully.
Which meant I hurtled into the room *un*gracefully,
Nellie the Elephant style.'

'Thank you!'

'Think nothing of it.' As if suddenly exhausted,
Jack dropped down on to the bed. He caught hold
of her hand and pulled her to sit beside him. 'The
porter conveyed he was more than willing to come
quietly, unlike some people who go around yelling
blue murder. Don't hurt me,' he begged, when she
made as if to dig him in the ribs. 'I escorted him
down to reception where I spoke to the manager.
Fortunately his English is good, so I was able to
explain what had happened. The manager pro-
ceeded to go berserk, the porter broke down in
tears and——'

Her face fell. 'He didn't? Oh, that's dreadful.'

'Don't you dare start feeling sorry for him,' Jack
rebuked. 'Apparently he has a penchant for spying

on young ladies, so he's no member of the League of Decency. He wasn't attempting to enter your room, just intending to peep through the keyhole. He'd been using the knob to steady himself as he crouched down and somehow disturbed the locking device. When you moved close—doubtless making all his fantasies come true,' Jack added drily, 'he backed off. Next moment you'd opened the door. He heard the racket when you came round to my room, but as he didn't know whether or not you'd realised who it was, he decided to sit tight. He was on the point of sneaking off when I cornered him.'

'I never even knew there was a keyhole,' Neille said, digesting the information. 'He can't have seen much.'

'No?' The word had a husky quality. Jack's gaze had dropped from her face to where a pulse beat in the hollow at the base of her throat. His eyes moved lower to the breasts which swelled, firm and satiny, from their nest of black lace. He tore his look upwards. 'No, I don't suppose he did,' he agreed, very matter-of-fact. 'But as this was the second time he'd been caught in the act, the manager asked if we wanted to press charges.'

'You didn't?' she burst out.

He shook his head. 'In the same breath he told me about the porter's ailing wife and five kids, so I didn't have the heart. What I did do was demand he be removed from the premises.'

'Thanks.' Satisfied with the outcome, Neille gave him a teasing glance. 'For a tyrant from the SAS you're one heck of a pushover.'

'And how about you?' He placed his hands on her shoulders and steered her firmly backwards until she lay flat on the bed, with him sitting over her. 'You might have a big mouth and be a whizz at grievous bodily harm, Nellie Trenchard, but deep down I suspect you're a pushover, too.'

'Who's got a big mouth?' she enquired, gazing up into his eyes.

'You.' He raised a finger and slowly, tantalisingly outlined her lips. 'And it's beautiful and I want to kiss it.'

Neille could feel electricity in the air, sense the throb of his heart beating in unison with hers. The world had stopped turning. They were alone together, in Paris. His fingers were moving over her face, caressing her cheek, marvelling at the smoothness of her skin, brushing wisps of copper-gold from her brow.

'Hello,' Jack whispered.

'Hello.'

Something wonderful was happening. They were meeting for the first time as lovers. Caught in the eye of an emotional hurricane, there was a stillness, a waiting, a tension. It was a crucial moment which Neille wanted to savour. She wanted to be able to say, 'That was the moment when we fell in love,' and yet also she badly wanted what came next. She wanted his kiss, to feel his hands on her body, to know the thrust and energy of his maleness. He would be a powerful lover, uninhibited and complete. She wanted all of that, all of him.

'We mustn't,' he said, answering her unspoken plea. He pushed himself upright. 'Not yet. It isn't ethical.'

'You've kissed me before,' she murmured, running her fingertips slowly down his arm.

'Yes, and that wasn't ethical either.' Jack frowned. 'But if I kiss you now it won't stop there, we both know that.' He rubbed his forehead in a gesture of frustration. 'I knew I should've arranged for Derek to accompany you to Paris. It was obvious we'd be isolated, alone together, and I thought I could handle it. But even before the damned plane took off I knew I'd made a mistake.'

'Did you?'

'Why else do you think I was keyed up? You were flirting, fluttering those long luscious lashes of yours, and all I could think about was——' Jack raked his hair with a single sweep of his hand. 'And when I slapped your backside—God! Things turned upside down and inside out. It was supposed to be a punishment for you, but instead it was sheer torture for me. How near I was to rolling you over and embedding myself in you. He flung her a fierce look. 'Like now.'

A smile played on her lips. 'Then kiss me.'

'Don't try seduction,' he warned, but it sounded like a plea.

Neille's smile widened. 'Aren't you the man who threatened to move in?'

He nodded grimly. 'And you don't need to have majored in psychiatry to analyse that as wish fulfilment, pure and simple. But I'm not moving in because I'm not changing my principles. I don't mix business with pleasure.' Rising to his feet, Jack began to pace back and forth beside the bed like a wild animal in a very small cage. 'Watching you parading around today half naked has been hell. I've been in a constant state of arousal. Neille,' his voice cracked, 'I've never felt as strongly about anyone as I feel about you. Half the time I could belt you because you're so damned sassy, the other half I'm obsessed with wanting to rip off your clothes and make love so hard and so bloody long that you're begging me for mercy.'

'Begging you to stop?' Her mood had changed. She was no longer playing the temptress. The time for playing had gone. Her love for Jack was real and serious. 'But I'm begging you to start,' she said, with no thought other than what they both wanted.

'We mustn't.' Did she know how beautiful she looked, he wondered. Lying there with her copper-gold hair dishevelled across the pillow? The black silk she wore clung to her body like a second skin. A thin strap hung off one shoulder. If he tugged that strap lower a breast would be freed, a full round breast. Already its point was pushing wantonly upwards, as her breast would push into his palm. Her skin would be warm and faintly scented, soft to his lips. He wanted to kiss her mouth, her breasts, all of her. Wanted to make a sensuous journey around her body, caressing and probing until she cried out and clung, nails gouging his flesh as he penetrated her. Jack closed his eyes. 'No,' he said, his voice harsh. 'We mustn't. It isn't fair to Lewis.'

Neille pushed herself up on to one elbow. 'But Lewis and I are . . . nothing. I don't love him and he doesn't love me. Oh, he might think he does, but he's never seen me as a real person. All I am to him is a pretty doll, one he hopes will charm his business associates and add a touch of glamour to his life.'

The grey eyes narrowed. 'Then he's asked you to marry him?'

'Not yet, though he's dropped hints. Which I've ignored,' she stressed.

Jack stopped pacing. 'I thought you reckoned your friendship was spasmodic? Sounds a darned sight more if Lewis is working up to a proposal.'

'Look, as far as I'm concerned, it's not even a friendship.'

'Yet after two years you have regular dates?'

'*Spasmodic* dates, which don't mean anything to me.'

He heaved a sigh. 'OK.'

'What you and I do together isn't going to harm Lewis,' Neille coaxed, relieved to see her statement had been accepted.

'But it'd harm me, my opinion of myself. No matter how precarious this relationship of yours is, I'm employed by the guy right now and he trusts me. He deserves my honesty. No way am I making love to you behind his back. I don't go in for deception.' His blood was cooling and Jack could be businesslike. 'Tonight we'll remain apart, but first thing tomorrow I'll put in a call to Australia and explain what's happened.'

'You mustn't do that!' she exclaimed, suddenly stricken.

'Don't worry, I'll be the soul of diplomacy.' Two steadying hands covered her shoulders and Jack smiled down. 'Even if he's hostile at first— and who can blame him?—he'll come round, the same as anyone else. He's not the first guy to be asked to step aside. Lewis has to accept——' He located the right word. '—kismet. He won't be thrilled when he hears what's happened, but it's not as though we've committed any crime. The situation's awkward, that's all.' Jack was becoming more businesslike by the minute. 'I'll arrange not to bill him for my services; that'll make me feel better even if it does nothing for him. And if his reaction is to order Rea Safeguards off his premises——' He shrugged 'Perhaps that's for the best.'

Neille chewed at her lip. 'I don't want you to tell Lewis anything.'

'Why not? You mean you'd rather break the news yourself? You'll ring him tomorrow?'

'No. Not tomorrow.'

'Then when? I feel it's important we be totally honest about this.' Jack waited, but she said nothing. 'You'd prefer to delay things and tell him to his face next week?' he hazarded. She remained mute. 'You do agree we can't cheat, that the only way is to be frank?'

'I suppose so,' she mumbled.

'Why the reluctance?' Jack caught hold of her chin, tilting her head until she was forced to meet his eyes. 'Why are you holding back?' A muscle clenched in his jaw. 'Or am I on the wrong track altogether? Maybe I'm deluding myself again? Maybe because I've fallen for you, I'm just imagining you've fallen for me?'

'I have!' she cried. 'I think you're wonderful, but——' Her gaze skidded away from the grey eyes which seemed to be whipping at her soul like the winter wind. Neille felt chilled through and through. Everything was moving too fast. If she started to explain why a confrontation with Lewis must be avoided at all costs, she would have to explain the whole story and that would involve . . .

'But what?' he demanded, his fingers tightening like a clamp. 'But wonderful as I am, I was only supposed to enter your bed for one night or maybe two, it that it? And why make ripples over something as insignificant as Parisian frolics? My God! I should have taken more notice of what was written in those gossip columns.' He snatched his hand from her jaw. ' "Game for anything" was one phrase I seem to remember. And that just about sums you up.'

'That's not true! It's just that—that my dealings with Lewis are at a delicate stage,' Neille said unsteadily. 'Now is not the right time for——'

'Yeah!' He cut her short. 'I can imagine. An educated guess says you're on pins waiting for those hints to turn into a definite proposal, one you *won't* be ignoring. Do you reckon it could be timed for his glorious homecoming?'

'Yes, as a matter of fact, I do, but—but——' She was conscious of flailing around. 'But I don't love him and——'

'What does loving matter when you're being handed riches on a plate?' Jack sneered. 'Lewis might be a crashing bore, but you can't escape the fact that he's loaded.'

'I don't care about his money.'

'Then what do you care about?' he asked coldly.

'You!'

He folded his arms and glared. 'So ring Lewis and tell him.'

'It's not that simple,' Neille muttered.

'Nothing ever is.' He was shooting out words like poisoned darts. 'But if you wanted a little excitement on the side while you waited for Mr Mitchell to pop the question, you came to the wrong man. A few years ago I regret to say I'd probably have obliged, but not now. The prospect of a one night stand or some furtive affair leaves me cold.' In a single stride he was at the door, flinging it wide. 'Which means I'd be grateful if you'd get out of my room and stay out—permanently.'

'But Jack——' she protested.

'*Out.*'

CHAPTER EIGHT

RESERVES of acting skills needed to be dredged up in order for Neille to get through the next day. As someone who had previously turned a disparaging eye on females who whined and whimpered over broken love affairs, her instinct was to whine and whimper herself. There had been hard times in plenty with Simon, but her feelings for Jack were completely different. Simon had needed *her*, but *she* needed Jack. And now she had been trapped into alienating him. He might have journeyed with her to André's studio for the final session, and eaten meals alongside, but his presence was purely physical. Keeping conversation to a bare minimum, he refused to share whatever was going on inside his head. Not that you needed to be clairvoyant to guess the gist. In Jack's view she was the good-time girl whom the gossip columns had depicted, and he should have known better than to have been duped.

But once he heard the reasons why she could not afford to upset Lewis ahead of time, wouldn't he understand and relent? A week, just seven more days, and hopefully she would be able to give Jack a full explanation. Yet maybe a week would be too late? Neille's stomach churned. His love—it had been love, hadn't it?—was a new and fragile emotion which required cosseting, not placing on a shelf in cold storage. In a week his love might freeze to death!

Several times she came perilously close to spilling out the story, but loyalty had her rejecting the impulse. It wasn't just *her* story. The long-ago lapse which allowed Lewis his exclusive leverage over her had remained a closely guarded secret, and before she uttered a single word she was obliged to ask her father's permission. And asking premature permission was impossible. Approaching him would require certain revelations—her love for Jack, her lack of love for Lewis, and how she was currently involved in a high-wire act. At such revelations, her father would panic. The dread he had carried around for twenty years would rise again, like a spectre. She could not be so cruel as to subject him to that. So she must wait seven long days, after which, with luck, Lewis would make a voluntary exit from her life.

Saturday brought no sign of a thaw. In near silence they breakfasted, motored to Charles de Gaulle Airport, and caught the London flight. On the plane Neille brought out her blood-and-guts thriller, but received no jokey observation this time. Head down, she turned the pages at what were intended to be convincing intervals, but none of the words made sense. It was a relief when they landed and she could find solace in the activities of disembarking and collecting luggage, but in the taxi the strained silence resumed. They sat like strangers, studying the scenery through opposite windows. They scanned the countryside, the outskirts of London, and finally the suburbs.

'This is goodbye.' Jack poked out a hand as they turned the corner into her road. 'I'll drop you off and continue in the taxi to my place.'

Neille gazed at him. 'You aren't supposed to leave until tomorrow.'

'One night isn't going to make any difference,' he replied, abandoning his attempt at a formal farewell. 'I want to get home and unpack, visit the launderette, buy in food. By clearing the domestic side today, I can devote tomorrow to the office.'

'Tomorrow's Sunday.'

Despite his withdrawal, that he would wish to cut loose ahead of time had never crossed her mind, and now she felt bereft. It might only be one night—with him sleeping in the spare room and her along the landing—but at least he would be near. And while he was near she could cling to the hope, albeit a gossamer one, that his attitude might soften.

'Clever girl. And Sunday means I'll be in the office alone and free from the telephone. There's paperwork a mile high waiting for me, so tomorrow presents the perfect opportunity for tackling it. Next house,' he instructed the taxi driver, and when they stopped he reached across to open the door. 'Go along. I'll bring your case.' He joined her on the front step, holding out his hand a second time. 'Goodbye.'

'Shouldn't you check to see there aren't any mafiosi hiding under my bed?' Neille asked, pretending not to notice the gesture. Goodbye was too final, something to be avoided at all costs.

'Mafiosi?' She was allowed a glimpse of the Jack Rea grin which had the impudent creases at the corners of his mouth deepening seductively. 'Wasn't the Yellow Peril designated as Public Enemy Number One?'

'Someone *did* send those threats.'

'The taxi's waiting.'

'I'm going to ask around, make enquiries.'

His sigh was impatient. 'Nailing someone at this stage would be academic.'

'No, it would be justice. And that's apart from the satisfaction there'd be of knowing who was responsible. I don't like loose ends.' She saw he had lifted a hand to the taxi driver, indicating he'd be there. 'Jack, you can't be on guard against an assassin for a month and not even be *interested*.'

'I can. This month, for all its——' He hesitated. '—ramifications, was only a job, one of many I've undertaken over the years. Now it's done, and my only thought is to take the money and run.'

'You're a beast,' Neille ground out. She hated his coolness, his indifference, his insistence on leaving. And she hated being relegated to a mercenary consideration.

He smiled. 'I prefer pachyderm.' His smile disappeared. 'Sunbeam, it's best if we make a clean break, OK? You and I just aren't meant to be. If I should see you coming towards me in future I'll hide round a corner, and I'd appreciate it if you'd do the same.' He strode back to the taxi where he lifted a hand in a half salute. 'Goodbye.'

Neille sucked the end of her pen. 'Think hard. Who else could've gained access to the in-tray apart from——' She checked her notepad. '—Lewis's secretary, the mail clerk, any of the directors, your assistant and you?'

Mr Trenchard sighed. His daughter's detective work had begun hours earlier, immediately on her return from France. All afternoon she had been coming up with first one theory, then another.

Throughout dinner her questions about the day-to-day functioning of Mitchells' head office had come thick and fast and now, when he had been hoping to relax and watch television, she was determinedly making lists.

'The cleaners,' he said with reluctance, 'and all the people who work in the general office. Lewis's secretary acts as a buffer, but it wouldn't have been impossible for someone to sneak in.'

'How many work in the general office?'

'Ten.' He did a mental recount. 'Change that to twelve. Neille, the police have already made enquiries. I don't see that——'

'Half-hearted enquiries,' she declared. 'Jack told me they regarded the threats as very small potatoes, so it follows that all they'd do was go through the motions. And they aren't privy to inside information, like you.'

'What inside information?'

'Inter-company gossip, the comings and goings.' She adjusted her grip on her pen. 'Now, can you remember whether Lewis had any outside visitors on the day prior to discovery of the note?'

'No, I can't, though doubtless somebody would have called. He's a very busy fellow. But I don't keep a check,' Mr Trenchard protested. 'My office is way down the corridor.'

'Yet presumably some of the people who visit him will visit you at the same time?' Neille persisted.

'Well, yes.'

'And you keep a note of your visitors in your desk diary?'

'Well, yes.'

'And you're in the habit of bringing your diary

home?' He nodded. 'I'll get it.' Seconds later, it was open across her knees. 'There was an official from the VAT office—we can discount him—and Andrew Rice!' she said in surprise. 'Whatever did he want?'

Neille knew the young man personally. The son of Walter Rice, a crusty old character who had held the post of Chief Accountant at Mitchells' before her father, Andrew had taken her out a few times shortly after Simon's death. He had been a pleasant enough escort, if overly keen on promoting a man-about-town image. She well remembered how he had doused himself with sufficient cologne to asphyxiate an army. Their friendship had ended when a titled young lady had fallen into his sights. Andrew was nothing if not a social climber. Neille hadn't minded, indeed she hadn't been in a fit state to mind about anything much at the time, but she had been thrown over with mind-boggling speed.

'Andrew had other business in the building, but I can only presume it was courtesy which prompted him to call on me. He passed on the latest news about Walter,' Mr Trenchard explained. 'Poor blighter's been in and out of hospital all year with chest trouble.'

'I thought you and Walter Rice didn't get on too well?' she queried, for her father had always regarded the old man as something of an ogre.

'Walter never got on with anybody. His idea of comradeship was to give it you in the neck. But Andrew's a jovial fellow. I expect he likes to keep the social niceties alive.' Mr Trenchard gazed longingly at the television. 'You needn't put his name down on your list of suspects. He wouldn't go within miles of Lewis's office, fear of Walter would keep him away. The old man'd throw a fit if he suspected his son of fraternising with the enemy. He never could abide Lewis, always called him the whippersnapper behind his back. No, Andrew would've steered well clear. He's as much in awe of his father as anybody.'

'No Andrew.' Neille returned to her list. 'Can you give me the names of the people who inhabit the general office?'

'Now?' Her father groaned.

She took pity. 'Tomorrow will do,' she grinned, and shut her notepad.

'Thank heavens for that.' He crossed the living room to press the appointed button. 'Make it tomorrow afternoon,' he said, as the screen filled with colour. 'Mrs Dawson discovered a pocket calculator under the chest of drawers in the spare room; it obviously belongs to Jack. I thought I'd pop round to his office in the morning and hand it over.'

'I'll go,' Neille offered, a shade too quickly.

Rea Safeguards's offices were tucked away at the rear of a warehouse in an obscure little street in central London. She parked her father's saloon alongside a somewhat battered station wagon and walked across the yard. Neille actually attempted a saunter, in case Jack happened to be looking out, but a furtive glance at the building revealed no sign of life. For that she was grateful. Having set off in confident mood, the closer she came to confronting him, the more the conviction grew that she'd have done better to have stayed home. His definition of her visit would be that she was

chasing him and she wasn't—was she? She had
more pride than to resort to such tactics—didn't
she? What she was suffering were merely withdrawal symptoms, a kind of after-the-party down.
Grief, no matter who you'd been shackled to, after
a month you'd miss them—wouldn't you?

Her fingers closed around the slim black
calculator. She would simply post the instrument
through the letter box and beat a hasty retreat.
Neille sped over the final yards and thrust the
calculator forward, but the door which in-
corporated the brass-edged slit for which she had
been aiming, fell away. Her arm followed, and she
was bending as a tall figure in tan cords and white
sweater was revealed on the threshold. She stood
up straight.

'You were waiting behind the door!'

'Naturally. I'm in security, remember? I keep my
eyes and ears open, so when a car drives into my
yard I sit up and take notice. I recognised the
Rover as your father's.'

Beneath his grey gaze, she had become a trifle
short of breath. 'Um, you left this,' she said,
shoving the calculator at him.

'Thanks.'

'My pleasure.'

'Is that it?' asked Jack, as she swivelled. He
rested a shoulder against the door frame. 'Where's
my daily dose of abuse? Come on in and have a
coffee, there're some questions I'd like to ask.'

Neille hesitated, surprised to hear he was
prepared to talk. What had happened to them
making a clean break? To him hiding round
corners? Her spirits lifted. An invitation to coffee
sounded encouraging, though she hoped his

questions didn't mean he intended to interrogate her about Lewis again. Maybe not. Maybe they were just an excuse to offer the hand of friendship. Maybe he regretted his heated accusations of the other evening and wanted to apologise?

Accepting with what was intended to be blithe indifference, she followed him down a passageway into a small bright office painted in toffee and white. It was a bit spartan, but the wooden floor was spotless. Filing cabinets lined one wall, while another was hung with a map of the British Isles. The paperwork which demanded his attention was stacked in neat piles on a scrubbed pine desk.

Jack indicated she was to be seated, then frowned. 'What on earth are you wearing?' he asked, stripping her down and reassembling her in a second. 'Cast-offs from a Mongolian peasant? What is it, one size fits all?'

'This is fashion!' she retorted indignantly, glancing down at the panels of pale fur which had been tossed over a suede tabard, which in turn covered leather gaucho pants. Cinnamon-brown boots, wrinkled at the ankles, completed the outfit. It was a November morning with a bite in the air, and Neille believed herself appropriately dressed.

Jack walked over to a table which did duty as kitchen, and plugged in an electric kettle. 'If that's standard gear for sleuthing I'd better tip Brian the wink. Poor guy's been slumming it in blue serge, but maybe it's time he skinned himself a few skunks. You take coffee with milk and one sugar. Right?'

'Right. Who says I'm sleuthing?' Neille demanded, wishing she could fathom his mood. He wasn't hostile, yet equally he did not appear to be going all out to make amends.

'When I departed yesterday weren't you attempting to con me into believing no stone would remain unturned in your search for our old friend, the assassin?' he countered, spooning instant coffee into two mugs.

'It wasn't a con.' Neille refused to admit, even to herself, that the idea had been originally voiced as a ploy to detain him a few moments longer. 'I've already made some enquiries.'

'And what pertinent clues have resulted?' he challenged.

'Um.' She blinked. 'Um—that Andrew Rice visited Mitchells' offices the day before the note surfaced.'

Jack filled the mugs with boiling water. 'Who's Andrew Rice?' She told him. 'And how do you know he was there?' She told him that, too. 'And what was this other business which needed his attention in the building?'

There Neille came unstuck. 'I don't know,' she admitted, taking the mug he handed her.

'What line's this Rice guy in?'

'He's a partner in a snooty art gallery in Mayfair. It specialises in imported icons, that kind of thing.'

Jack's nose twitched. 'The perfect accessory for the Mongolian peasant, but hardly department store merchandise?'

'No,' she agreed, watching him sit in the chair behind the desk and stretch out his legs. Why *had* Andrew visited Mitchells'? she wondered. Hadn't his father left breathing fire and brimstone, and swearing never to set foot on the premises again, and wasn't Andrew the obsequious son? 'Maybe I should pay him a visit?' she said, thinking out loud.

'And say what? "You, Andrew Rice, are the assassin, and I, Neille Trenchard, claim my reward"?'

'Okay, Jackson Rea,' she retorted. 'What would you do?'

'Nothing. A fundamental rule in the security game is that, before you take aim and fire, you make very sure you're looking at the right target. Marching into someone's home and asking them to incriminate themselves could easily wind up with you being slung out on your ear.'

'Never!'

Jack gave an amused grunt. 'No, in your case I tend to agree. Chances are you'd flatten anyone who so much as waved an admonishing finger. But to be serious, you need much more to go on. And if you ever do have real suspicions, and not just something which has come straight off the top of your head,' he thrust, 'you must go to the police.' Jack drank a mouthful of coffee, then leant forward to frown at a folder which lay open on his desk. 'Now, question number one—was Simon Gates a drug addict?'

Neille gasped, jerking back as if he'd thrown his mug of hot coffee straight into her face. She had believed the past safely buried, six feet under, but here was Jack, ruthlessly and unexpectedly demanding exhumation. Her heart sank. Her blood ran cold. She had not been invited into his office to receive apologies. On the contrary. Having classed her as a money-grabbing minx, now he seemed intent on amassing further evidence against her! She knew enough about people's prejudices to know that if you associated with a drug user you were considered suspect yourself.

'I've been reading these press cuttings again,' he explained, calmly sorting out various pieces of paper. 'This time I read between the lines. Gates's behaviour meant he either had to be a screwball, or hyped up on coke or something stronger. And I doubt you'd associate with a screwball.'

'I've associated with *you*,' she shot back. Neille squared her shoulders. 'Does it state anywhere in those cuttings that Simon was on drugs?'

He sighed. 'You know the answer to that. No, not in black and white. But with a captain of industry for a father and a popular actress for a mother, money can't have been in short supply. Cash can buy——' Jack frowned. 'If not complete silence, at least a certain discretion.' His eyes had never left her face. 'So—was he a drug addict?'

'Yes!' She lashed the answer at him like a wounded animal. 'Yes, yes, he was! Happy now?'

'Question number two. The official version is that he died of a mystery illness, but did he commit suicide?'

Neille's head went down. Despite the covering of suede and fur, she shivered, racked with private pain. 'Does it matter?'

'Yes, it does,' Jack replied firmly.

'Why?' She tossed a rich strand of hair from her shoulder, meeting his look with burning blue eyes. There was a feeling of *déjà vu*. Once before he had asked a question, and once before she had met it point-blank by asking what she asked now. 'Why should it matter to you?'

'Shall we just say I'm interested in people, in what they do and why? Being a bodyguard can be an unenviable mix of tedium and tension, but if nothing else it provides ample opportunity for the study of human behaviour.'

The feeling of *déjà vu* persisted. This time Jack was using phrases like 'studying human behaviour' whereas last time he had mentioned 'compiling a dossier'. But weren't they part of the same syndrome—rank curiosity!

'As a self-taught psychiatrist you'd like to study Simon's case history?' Neille's tone was bitter.

'And yours.'

His cool was unnerving. Wasn't it enough to have classed her as shoddy goods without now wanting to poke around further? And to think, this was the man to whom she had been prepared to reveal her father's secret. She had imagined Jack to be—special. He wasn't special, he was one of a multitude who, under the guise of being 'interested in people', fed like vultures on the mistakes and misfortunes of others. He would set himself up as judge and jury, too. It had been done before. Neille's eyes hardened. If he wanted a juicy exposé, one for which the gutter press had offered thousands, she would provide a blow by blow account, in lurid detail. Jack had once spoken of climbing into the mind—well, catch, boyo! Here come the ropes, the cleats, a pick-axe.

'No, Simon didn't commit suicide; he died of an overdose. But, to you, that probably amounts to the same thing!'

'How did you meet?'

'Through my cousin, Paul. They were in the same house at school. Paul was a day boy, Simon boarded. When Simon was expelled—for *smoking pot*,' Neille said, with a virulent flourish, 'he came to stay with us.'

'Why?' Legs spread, Jack looked very laid back.

'Because there was nowhere else for him to go,' she blitzed, 'and Mooie took pity on him. She adopts waifs and strays, like me!' She shot him a glance to see his reaction, but he was sipping coffee. 'Simon's parents had been divorced a couple of years earlier, and as his real mother was off on a European tour and his stepmother habitually raised three cheers when he went out the door rather than in, Mooie offered a haven. Simon had got himself expelled weeks away from sitting his final exams, and she arranged for him to study at home, then return to sit the papers at school. In the event, he gained a place at university. You won't find a mention there,' she flashed, when Jack shuffled through the cuttings. 'Simon packed it in after a couple of terms. Three more years of study wasn't what he wanted.'

'What did he want?'

'He didn't know.' Her chin lifted. 'But who does know at nineteen?'

'Wouldn't it be easier if you cut down on the aggro?' Jack suggested. 'I'm not holding a loaded gun at your head. Hell, I've made enough of a cock-up of my own life to hesitate before firing bullets.'

Lower lip thrust out, Neille regarded him warily. He had spoken with the voice of reason, but what did that conceal? Some of the reporters in her past had sounded reasonable, and the very next day had done a hatchet job.

'In next to no time Simon was knocking on my aunt's door again,' she continued, using a slightly less embattled tone, 'and she readopted him. His looks and charm were a formidable combination, and when he asked if he could stay for the summer, Mooie agreed. She was always ruffling his hair and telling him he looked like an angel. No one could have guessed he was destined to turn into a devil,' she added bleakly. She drew a breath, almost a sigh. Maintaining full tilt aggression had become wearisome now she had been sucked into telling her tale. 'In those days Simon was good-mannered and good fun. I'm sure he never used drugs in Sussex. If he had, Mooie would've slung him out, for all she had a soft spot. At first I was just . . . intrigued. Simon was so different from my cousins. They're sturdy types, brick walls emotionally, but he was vulnerable. He didn't wear his heart on his sleeve, it was more subtle than that, but you could sense a kind of inward cry for help. He was always so damned grateful for any kindness,' Neille added, with a sudden spark of anger. 'He found work on a nearby farm, and he and I began spending time together. We used to wander through the fields and talk and talk and talk. Nothing was held back. I suppose we were drawn together because neither of us had had what you'd call the regulation family. I mean, I know I was loved, but I wasn't Mooie's real child, was I?' She blinked. 'And Simon had never even been loved.'

'He was when you came along,' Jack pointed out softly.

'Yes.' Her throat felt hard. 'Yes. Though for a long time it was boy and girl stuff, completely innocent.'

'Where do his parents fit into this?' he asked, when she sat staring down at the mug in her hands.

'They supported him financially, period. As ambitious egotists, Mr and Mrs Gates did their own thing and to hell with everyone else, including their son. Simon had been brought up by a succession of nannies and au pairs. He'd never known a stable, loving family life.'

'And as a salve to their consciences, his parents provided sufficient cash for him to support a drug habit?'

'He was a pusher's delight.' Neille gave a laugh which sounded suspiciously like a sob. 'But that came later. Everything went fine that golden summer until his mother completed her tour and swooped down. She insisted Simon should move into her London flat. She bought him lots of new clothes, a car, and introduced him to the champagne set. Then she disappeared again. A little later I left Sussex and came to live with my father, so Simon and I took up where we'd left off. But in the city environment everything seemed ... faster. He insisted our love affair become the real thing.'

'Did you move in with him?'

'Grief, no. Despite a rapidly acquired gloss, beneath it I was gauche. And my father would've been horrified. Though I caused him enough heartache as it was,' she said regretfully.

Jack fingered the cuttings. 'These make you out as quite a girl for discos and all-night parties.'

'Initially, I was. I had no friends in London, so naturally I gravitated towards Simon's crowd. They were attention seekers—I suppose Simon was, too; smoking pot was a manifestation of that—and the idea was to project a high profile. At first I joined in. I kidded myself that acting up was the sophisticated way to behave.'

'You'd be eighteen, and adrift after being cut loose from your childhood ties?' Neille nodded. 'I imagine your father wasn't much of a disciplinarian?'

'If only he had been! But he watched on in despair while I went my own silly way.'

'Pity I wasn't around to administer a damned good spanking,' Jack remarked.

She gave a rueful smile. 'Where were you when I needed you?'

'Kicking over the traces myself, regrettably. So there you were, painting the town red with young Lochinvar?'

Neille nodded. 'That's how the gossip columns got wind of us. Simon had a taste for trendy places where a photographer's in perpetual attendance, and due to his parentage and looks he was a natural. As his companion, I also rated a line or two.'

He lifted a cutting. 'You remind me of those glamorous people in Martini ads.'

'It felt like that,' she confessed, 'until I came down to earth. Then I realised I didn't care for the people I was mixing with, and that there had to be more to life than laughing like a drain at rowdy parties. I began to back-pedal and tried to persuade Simon to do the same. He wasn't having any.' Neille heaved a sigh. 'That left me torn. I wanted to be with him, but not with his associates. I cut down on visiting "in" places, though the press never noticed. I was described as "party loving" when I'd stayed home at night for months. And Simon chugged along surrounded by sycophants.'

'Did he go out to work?'

'Off and on. His father fixed him up with a job as sales rep with one of his companies, but he never took it seriously. His lack of ambition used to drive me wild. Yet what impetus did he have when he was living the life of Reilly on handouts?'

Jack pushed the photograph back into the folder. 'Had the drug habit taken hold?'

She nodded. 'It was the usual thing, first cocaine for kicks, then the move to heroin and a multitude of other substances. I'd always been critical of those crazy enough to indulge, so for a full year or more he pretended he wasn't addicted, then——' Her eyes were stinging with tears. '—then there were needle marks on his arm. I did my best to get him to seek professional advice, to attend a drug dependence clinic, and he went along for a few times, but——' She raised and dropped her hands. '—he blew it. He always did. There were so many false hopes, so many broken promises. He was like a flame, burning himself up and scorching everyone else around him. The downs which followed his sprees left him moody, and impotent, and sometimes violent,' Neille remembered.

Jack straightened. 'Did Gates hit you?'

'No, he never laid a finger on me, though he punched other people. It was as a result of him punching a reporter that the gossip column write-ups became character assassinations. Get on the wrong side of the press, and they retaliate. I'd always been written up as a winky-pink girl, but overnight I became a tramp.' Neille looked him in the eye. 'Game for anything.'

Jack looked back steadily. 'I apologise for that. And you stuck with Gates to the end?'

'Who else did he have? Oh, I often told him it was over. That he needn't bother calling until he'd straightened himself out, but Simon only had to lift the phone and I rushed round.' The tears were stinging again. 'Your twenty-four-carat gold pushover.'

'That's what love does for you.'

The tenderness she heard in his voice almost made her sob out loud. She had never found anyone willing to listen, and though she accepted his interest as prurient, he did sound sympathetic. Her father had never sympathised, he simply preferred not to know, and Lewis had not even had the grace to acknowledge that Simon had ever walked this earth.

'There wasn't much love left at the end.' Neille gave a loud sniff. 'Love became pity. Having a rapport with a person who's either high as a kite or vomiting over the sink, is difficult.' She found a handkerchief and blew her nose, then she scoured him with a look. 'You might like to make a note in your dossier to the effect that the photograph of me swimming naked was actually taken when I was in the throes of trying to stop Simon from disgracing himself. Yet another occasion when he blew it.'

'Go on,' Jack prompted, when she stopped and glared.

'We were on holiday in Italy. I thought that if I could get him away from his cronies for a week or two, I'd be able to wean him off the drugs. Just shows how naïve I was,' she said, using a brittle voice. 'But the very first night I was awoken by the commissionaire knocking on my door. I couldn't understand him, but rapidly gathered it had

something to do with Simon causing a disturbance. I'd pulled on a robe to answer the door
and, because the man was so insistent that I hurry,
I set off with him down the staircase and out to
the fountains at the front of the hotel. There I
found Simon, fully dressed, wading around up to
his waist. He was stoned out of his mind. At
intervals around the pool were bronze fish
spouting water, and he was standing first under
one, then under another, singing at the top of
his voice. I begged him to get out and go to his
room, but he advised me to take a running
jump, or something similar.' Neille could not
prevent a small smile. 'Guests had begun to
gather, toffee-nosed and scandalised, and I grew
desperate. I tried to grab him, but couldn't get a
proper grip, and the commissionaire refused to
help because he didn't want his clothes wet, so I
climbed in. Simon thought that was great.'

'I can imagine. Communal bathtime.'

Her smile broaded. 'It was dreadful then, but
now I can see the comic aspect. Simon began to
undress, and as fast as he took something off, so I
tried to get it back on him. He kept falling over in
the water, standing up and sitting down, and in the
struggles my robe became untied. Simon realised it
before I did, and he gave one great whoop of joy
and ripped the robe clean off. I went down with a
splash!'

Jack picked out a cutting. 'And at that precise
moment someone in the crowd took a photograph.'
He grinned. 'Here you are, wearing an astonished
look and nothing else.'

'Yes, well.' The sight of his proof changed her
mood. Comic or not, that night had been

purgatory. Like the months which had followed. Like Simon's death.

'And the press had a field day?'

She resented being nudged along. 'You've read it all, you know their reaction,' she thrust, rising from her chair. This interrogation must stop, she needed to get away. 'As you've guessed, Simon's father stepped in, terrified his son might be labelled in public as a drug addict, and he did manage to suppress an outright declaration. But his dependency was an open secret. And now *you* know that secret,' Neille said belligerently, throwing daggers with her eyes.

Attack was vital. It held at bay tears which, once again, were threatening to fall. She had given Jack the truth, she would not give him anything else. Neille Trenchard would never be so pathetic or self-indulgent as to sob on the shoulder of an interrogator. Flinging a fur panel across her chest, she marched to the door. She had intended to spear him to the spot with a challenging look, the final gesture of defiance, but when she turned her eyes were blurred. She rushed out into the passageway. A dam had been breached, already her cheeks were wet. Two long years of repressed pain and hurt were flooding out. She needed to be alone. To cry for Simon and herself.

'Sunbeam, wait,' she heard him call, but she rushed blindly on.

CHAPTER NINE

THE dawning of Monday meant her life had returned to normal, or so Neille told herself. She went into the agency and, after reporting back on her Paris assignment, received details of the bookings and interviews which had been arranged for the week. Her days were jam-packed. Good. The less time available for dwelling on her relationships with both Jack and Lewis, the better. The first had already crumbled, the second soon would—given luck. But until Friday her 'good friend' needed to be kept at a distance. Neille made plans accordingly, and when the phone rang in the evening and a clipped voice announced that Lewis Mitchell had returned to home base, she was prepared.

'I hope you had a good trip,' she said pleasantly.

'Most rewarding.' He used her comment as a springboard from which to dive into a numbing résumé of what had been happening to him over the past month, and by the time he got around to asking, 'How's life been treating you?' Neille was glassy-eyed. She leapt to attention, only to discover Lewis had moved on to a lecture. 'I'm not one to point a finger, but I'd have appreciated some first-hand contact, instead of having to rely on Jack Rea's reports that you were fighting fit. However,' he sighed, relishing his martyrdom, 'I'm back, and neither of us have been bundled off by some maniac with an axe to grind.'

'All's well that ends well,' she agreed, and the prosaic comment sufficed. Lewis never required much participation, and especially not over the phone. Each call was conducted like a business meeting, with him in charge at the head of the table.

'True, true. Now, next on the agenda is us getting together.'

'I'm afraid I'm booked up tomorrow night,' Neille inserted on cue. 'The agency requested I attend an important perfume promotion, and there was no way I could wriggle out.' She crossed her fingers as she lied.

'Never worry,' he said, displaying unusual magnanimity. 'I'm tied up tomorrow myself. Actually, I'll be out of town until late Thursday. Staff from various branches appear to have ganged up, and the ringleaders need to be shown the errors of their ways.' He heaved the sigh of someone crawled over by unruly infants. 'You and I will get together on Friday,' he decreed. 'We'll make it a special occasion, so wear something long and pretty.'

Special occasion. Neille knew what that meant—his dreaded proposal. The jitters suddenly attacked. She was cutting everything very fine. Suppose the lingerie photographs didn't do the trick, what then? There was no way she could agree to marry the man. She *must* refuse him. But how could she turn him down without exciting hostility? Lewis's puffed-up opinion of himself guaranteed he would take offence—and seek revenge. The fingers gripping the receiver drained white. She wasn't the one who would stand in the firing line, her father made a natural target.

'I'll ring early evening Friday to finalise details,' Lewis continued, and made his clipped farewells.

Afterwards Neille stood, hands pressed to her cheeks, and sighed. Then her chin lifted. She would not be so defeatist as to spend each free minute between now and Friday wallowing in gloom. Not that there'd be many free minutes for her evenings, as well as her days, had been filled with painstaking care. But Lewis's absence now meant she was landed with the perfume shindig, a health shop opening and a cosmetic launch. Each promised to be dull. Should they be abandoned? On reflection, she decided to go along. The events would be a bulwark against her 'good friend' changing his mind and requesting an earlier meeting.

When the phone rang ten minutes later, she congratulated herself on her wisdom. This must be Lewis, already having second thoughts. Neille brushed off her excuses and stood them in line.

'Hello?' she said cautiously.

'Hi, it's Jack. Are you free tomorrow evening?'

Jack! Irritation mingled with dismay, yet interspliced was a hefty dose of excitement. Excitement? Only a dimwit would continue to be attracted by a man who made no bones about regarding the intimate details of her life purely as an exercise in human behaviour.

'Tomorrow?' she gasped, as if he had grabbed her by the throat.

'Yes. You see, after our talk I decided I wanted to know more about——'

He wanted to know more! He had further questions to ask! How cold-blooded and analytical and downright nosy could anyone be? Neille squeezed her eyes tight shut. Didn't he care that she had left his office shaking and shivering after facing up to her past? Her emotions heaved and bucked. Lewis displayed the sensitivity of a rhinoceros, but Jack was ten times worse.

'You can't,' she muttered. 'You can't see me tomorrow.' She snatched back her composure to speak coldly and clearly. 'I have an important engagement which I'm not in the least inclined to cancel. Good night.'

Sparing no expense, for the evening was tax deductible, the perfume company had booked a suite in a luxury hotel on Park Lane. Gold-edged invitations had been distributed like confetti, hundreds of give-away sample bottles containing two drops of their spectacular new fragrance laid on, and prayers offered up that more than three dozen stalwarts might deign to attend. By seven o'clock their staff were in place, smiles at the ready. By seven-thirty, the smiles had begun to droop. They revived at seven forty-five when a cluster of buyers wandered in, then sagged five minutes later when they departed.

At eight o'clock, Neille was walking up the hotel steps when she felt her arm being gripped from behind. She turned, then froze, frowning at her captor on the step below.

'If it isn't my favourite Mongolian,' grinned Jack, his eyes swooping up and down in swift appraisal. 'Funny, but on second inspection that outfit looks great.'

Irritably, she shook his hand away. He looked pretty great himself, camel coat over dark suit, but she had no intention of reacting to his undoubted sex appeal.

'Would you kindly stop hounding me?' she demanded. 'I'm busy. Didn't I make it clear I have a very important function to attend this evening?'

'You lied.'

'Did I?' Her eyes became glittering sapphires. 'Then let me tell you something. I'm getting very tired of——'

'You look terrific. Your creamy complexion against that fur—mmm.'

She cold-shouldered the compliment. 'See here, zonko, your little cross-eyed friend may have told you where to find me this evening, but she did you no favours because in coming here you've wasted your time.'

'Like you intend to waste yours, eating curled up canapés, drinking boxed wine, and all to the accompaniment of rhubarb-rhubarb conversation?'

'I'd rather do that than listen to you asking more of your damned questions!' she retorted, in fire-breathing style.

Jack re-established his grip. 'No questions. Answers.'

'About what?' she asked suspiciously, as he began propelling her down the steps towards his station wagon. Neille wished the doorman wasn't showing such an interest. If they hadn't been overlooked she would have given Jack a sharp kick on the shins, and marched off into the night. But such behaviour within the confines of an upmarket hotel seemed scarcely ladylike.

'About Andrew Rice and the threats.'

'You've been to see him?' she enquired, unable to keep from being intrigued.

Jack nodded. 'In view of your comments on

Sunday, I decided he was worth a visit.' He opened the passenger door. 'Hop in.'

'But you said——'

He walked to the other side of the car. 'I know what I said. Look, Neille, I'm parked on double yellow lines so you're going to have to make up your mind whether you're getting in or not.'

'Are we visiting the Rice household?'

'No, I'm taking you home. I did fix for us to visit young Mr Rice this evening, but he rang me an hour ago. Seems he got cold feet. The prospect of meeting one of the injured parties proved too embarrassing. He asked if I'd pass on the full facts, plus apologies.'

'Then he *is* involved in the threats?'

'He delivered them.'

Neille's brows lifted. Her suspicions had been embryo suspicions at best, expected to be stillborn, but here the young man's involvement was, alive and kicking.

'What's he got against Lewis?' she asked, climbing into the car.

'Nothing.' Jack accelerated away. 'The threats were contained in an envelope, which he believed contained a trade article praising Mitchells' chief competitor. That's what his father had told him when he gave instructions for the envelope to be tucked amongst papers in the in-tray. Walter also instructed Andrew that he was to sneak in between one and two when Lewis's secretary would be at lunch, and to make certain he wasn't observed. Being under his father's thumb, he agreed to act as messenger boy. Mind you, he did regard bringing the article to Lewis's attention as a bit of a jape. To paraphrase, he knew Mitchell's inflated opinion of himself and the way he runs his company, so the prospect of him throwing a tantrum was not displeasing.'

'I bet it was Andrew who threw the tantrum when he discovered he'd delivered a threatening letter!'

'But he didn't discover. His connection with Mitchells' is slight, so no news filtered through from there, and although he did come across a pencilled note last weekend which, when he showed it to me, I recognised as a facsimile, the penny didn't drop.'

'But if he'd read the threats surely he should have queried them with his father?'

'That would have been difficult.' Jack paused. 'Considering Walter Rice died ten days ago.'

'Daddy never said.'

'He didn't know until I broke the news this afternoon.' He flung her a sideways glance. 'Your father and I shared a very long and very interesting conversation. And it was he who informed me of your whereabouts, not Dee. Daddy never said that either, did he?' he mimicked, and grinned when he saw her lips had jammed together. 'Yes, not satisfied with one stool pigeon I've recruited a second—in family.'

'It was obvious from the start you hold nothing sacred,' Neille retaliated. She looked out through the windscreen. 'And you said you were taking me home, but this isn't the way.'

'Yes, it is. To *my* home. You needn't worry, I've told your father you'll be spending the evening with me and be perfectly safe.'

'Huh!' The trouble was, she did not know whether she wanted to be safe or not. 'So Andrew only realised what had happened when you arrived?'

'That's right. Bearing in mind the bad blood between his father and Lewis, he'd taken the pencil note to be wishful thinking, like sticking pins into a wax doll. He was quite perturbed when I informed him otherwise! Then he explained how his father had been so anti-Lewis that every single change made in the department stores was decried. The old man was particularly incensed when the sale of liquor was introduced, which seems to be the reference to old values being trampled underfoot.'

Neille frowned. 'Did Mr Rice ever intend to act on the threats?'

'That would've been impossible. He had such difficulty with his breathing that simply moving from one room to another wore him out. I spoke to Brian, Detective Inspector Gilchrist, this morning, and he verified that. He'd interviewed Walter, obviously when Andrew was at work, and remembered how frail the old man was. He'd eliminated him from police inquiries straight away.'

She sighed. 'So the only thing we still don't know is why that photograph accompanied the threats?'

'I think we do.' Jack turned into a tree-lined avenue. 'When I mentioned the photo it was the first Andrew knew of it and initially he was perplexed. Then, with a very red face, he confessed he might be to blame. It seems that when you and he had those few dates two years back, his father had been pleased, and——'

'But I only met him a couple of times, and on

each occasion he growled at me like an old bear,'
Neille interrupted.

'Well, apparently he liked you, reckoned you
had spunk.' Jack twitched his nose. 'And I confess
I agree. However, Andrew met the Honourable
Miss So-and-so, and—not to put too fine a point
on it—dumped you. Because he knew there'd be
hell to pay if his lack of chivalry was revealed, he
told Walter *you'd* dumped *him*.' There was a
pregnant pause. 'For Lewis. Which guaranteed
you were flavour of the month.'

'And by including my photograph Mr Rice had
a dig at me!'

'Seems like it,' he agreed, swinging the station
wagon off the avenue and through an archway
into a small courtyard. On three sides were mews
houses, built of a stone which gleamed pale in the
moonlight. There were balconies and flower boxes,
and fir trees stood like sentries beside front doors.
'Andrew was apologetic, embarrassingly so.'

'He won't get into trouble, will he?'

'No, o lady of the soft heart, he won't.' Jack
pulled to a halt beside a porch, and switched off
the engine. 'Brian is to have a quiet word with
Lewis to explain, and then the file'll be closed.'

'Good,' she said, as he helped her out. 'Does
Andrew still go heavy on the cologne?'

'Heavy? My sinuses were cleared in thirty
seconds.' He wobbled his head. 'When he was
blabbering his apologies he had his arm around
my shoulders, and the smell almost had me
passing out. He kept saying how sorry he was it'd
all happened—not that I am—and——'

'I beg your pardon?'

'I'm not.' Jack was searching in his trouser

pocket for the front door key. 'I'm not sorry it happened.'

'You're not sorry!' Neille could hardly believe her ears. How selfish could anyone be? Lifting an enraged finger, she jabbed it towards him. 'Well, I *am* sorry, zonko! In Paris I believed myself to be in danger of being hung, drawn and quartered by whoever wrote those threats, and even though it turned out I was being pursued by a fan-worshipping oriental, I was still frightened.' She began to poke her finger into his camel-coated chest. 'But *you* weren't sorry then, like *you* aren't sorry now. What concerns *you* is filthy lucre. *You* have no finer feelings. All *you* care about is taking the money and running!'

'*Wrong!*' he shot back, so fiercely that Neille jumped. His index finger was raised. 'I care about a lot of things, one of which happens to be *you*. That's why I'm not sorry, because without Walter Rice and his threats I'd never have met *you*.' Now Jack was emphasising with pokes. 'And *you* happen to be driving me crazy with unrequited lust. And *you* can damned well give me a kiss.'

Thrusting his hand to the back of her head, he grabbed her against him with such force that their mouths met in an abrupt fusion of heat, surprise and longing. Neille's eyelids fluttered closed. His fingers were gripped tight among the torrent of shiny hair, but after that first kiss imprisonment was unnecesary. Enchanted by the need in him, the taste of his mouth, the pressure of his lips, she welcomed this intrepid invasion. One kiss became two, three, four, each slightly gentler and more persuasive than the last. He was nibbling with a half-opened mouth, seducing her, taming her, letting her know who was the master. When eventually Jack raised his head, she drew in a breath which was not quite a cry, not quite a sigh. The chemistry of his kisses was potent. Neille wasn't sure how she came to be wrapped so slavishly around him, but, if she was driving him crazy, he had her completely bewitched.

'Don't stop,' she murmured.

'I'd better. Unless you want my neighbours complaining that we're causing a public disturbance.'

'I do.'

'You would.' He finally got around to unlocking the front door. 'Come inside. We'll continue our talk, have a drink and maybe . . . horizontal bliss?'

Neille went ahead of him into the living room furnished with cool blond wood and white carpets. Like his office, it was on the spartan side, but the bareness had been relieved by the deft deployment of plants. Busy Lizzies tumbled from hanging pots, ferns grew in corners, ivies fell from pine shelving.

'I thought if I wanted a little excitement I'd come to the wrong man,' she teased.

'You have.' He went into the kitchen. 'I intend to give you one hell of a lot of excitement. But all the things I said about Parisian frolics etc.,—well, I guess you must blame my hormones.' He stood in the doorway, smiling at her. 'I was so damned frustrated when you started belly-aching about keeping Lewis in the dark, that something inside of me exploded. Sunbeam, you were so bloody *insistent*.'

Neille's happiness nose-dived. How could she get involved with Jack while her 'good friend' hovered like an ominous shadow?

'I still am,' she muttered.

'But maybe everything changes on Friday?'

Her eyes opened wide. 'How do you know that?'

'I worked things out.' Jack appeared to have forgotten about organising drinks. 'Now I'm half-way to understanding about you and Lewis. Don't forget, I've spoken to your father.'

'But Daddy doesn't know about Friday, and he would never tell——' She bounced back like a wrestler off the ropes. 'You had no right to speak to him!'

'I had every right. I love you, that gives me the right. And you've been protecting him far too long.'

'Have I?' Neille was busily working through the implications. Jack had said he loved her, and that was wonderful, because she loved him. But ... 'What did my father say?' she demanded.

'That he'd allowed you to cope with Lewis alone for far too long.'

'Cope with Lewis? He said that?' She frowned. 'But I thought——'

'You thought your father genuinely believed the pair of you were good friends, despite all the evidence to the contrary?' Jack shook his head. 'He told me he'd taken the coward's way out and paid lip service. That he preferred to pretend all was well between you and Lewis, rather than face up to the truth. And I suspect you did a little pretending of your own?'

'I did,' she admitted. 'Daddy likes life smooth. Ripples upset him, so I never said anything to rock the boat.'

'And you and Lewis drifted on?'

'I did try and swim for the shore once,' she said,

with a rueful smile. 'Remember I explained how the dates began at a time when I felt numb? That I'd sit in my private daze when he put the marketing world to rights? Well, obviously in time the numbness began to wear off and one evening, about a year ago, something went snap! I saw what I'd lumbered myself with and realised I couldn't take much more. When Lewis rang to fix the next date, I refused. He rang again, and I manufactured another excuse. And again. Then he spoke to my father at the office.'

'And he went to pieces?'

Neille nodded. 'He rushed home in a dither, demanding to know what had gone wrong. When I said that all that had happened was I'd decided to call it a day because we had nothing going for us, he pleaded with me to give it time. He refused to see any reason why the courtship shouldn't continue. Courtship!' she exclaimed. 'That was Lewis's term. But the whole thing had been so damned tepid. There'd been long gaps between dates and Lewis's idea of being ardent was the odd fumbled kiss, so I couldn't see what all the fuss was about. I told my father I wasn't interested in a courtship, that I just wanted out and no hard feelings, but—but——' Neille suddenly clammed up. She had been rambling on, explaining with no thought of discretion, and now she realised her mistake. Even if Jack *did* love her, and even if he *had* spoken to her father, by his own admission he was only half-way to understanding the situation. Was she at liberty to reveal the rest? She wanted to, very badly, but . . .

'Your father begged you to think again,' Jack told her. 'He was afraid that if you offended Lewis there might be reprisals. Yes,' he said, when she shot him a startled look, 'he didn't go into details over the phone, but he did refer to a crime he'd committed a long time ago which he felt, and still feels, Lewis might resurrect and use against him. He said you would explain.'

'Daddy gave permission?'

For years the secret had remained hidden in the dark corners of her father's mind—Neille herself had only been allowed access twelve months ago when she had tried to kick loose, and then only because Mr Trenchard had seen no alternative—yet now he had handed it to Jack as a gift.

'He did, but do you think we could leave your explanations for later?' He came forward to enfold her in his arms. 'It's time we went upstairs.'

'But you said we were going to have a talk, a drink, and——'

'You have a nasty habit of quoting what I say back to me,' he murmured, bending to kiss and then nibble at her ear lobe. 'Now I've discovered my priorities were wrong. The sequence has been changed, my darling Mongolian. Horizontal bliss come first, so will you kindly get upstairs?'

Neille did as she was told. The bedroom, like the rest of the house, was pale wood and white, and in need of a woman's touch. Not that she had much time to notice, because as she removed one of her layers of fur, so Jack decided he had better remove another. The fur, followed by the suede, and finally the leather, fell to the bedroom floor, and as each inch of exposed flesh was gilded with kisses, so her surroundings diminished into a hazy blur. A tremor rippled through her. All that mattered was this lovely man who was making the heat, such exquisite heat, begin to glow. His fingers on her skin had weighted her breasts with heavy languor, filled her blood with a throbbing urgency. No longer a glow, the heat began to smoulder as his kisses, at first gentle and seductive, became an impassioned searching which had her straining to respond.

'Oh!' Neille sucked in a breath as his lips brushed across a rose-brown nipple, stiffened with want. 'Oh!' she groaned again, as the warm moist tug of his mouth on her breast sent arrows of need shooting down. 'Oh, no!' she pleaded, as he left her. But he was quickly back, naked and muscled and eager for love.

'Hello,' Jack murmured, smiling into her eyes.

'Hello.'

'I love you,' he said, and began kissing her again, long lingering kisses.

'And I love you.'

His mouth moved to her breast again, his tongue capturing the rose-brown peak in a way which made her groan, had her back arching. From smouldering, she had burst into flame. Neille had never felt so tender, so aroused, so aware of herself as a woman designed to please a man. And such a wonderful man.

'Did you know the navel is this season's erogenous zone?' he enquired, kissing her stomach. He raised his eyes to grin. 'I read it in one of your fashion books.' Next Jack caressed her thigh. 'But how about here? And here, and——' There was a pause as his fingers slithered down. 'Here?'

'Yes, please yes.'

His mouth and his hands were shooting sparks in all directions. How could he give her so much

pleasure, and how could she return it? She wanted
to touch him like he was touching her, run her
hands over his shoulders, his back, through his
hair. Close her fingers around the proud male
muscles.

'Oh, sunbeam,' he moaned, as she began her
exploration.

Jack's body was lean and hard, his skin
glistening with a faint sheen. He lay still while she
rubbed her mouth against the curly black hair on
his chest, then moved, trapping her beneath him.
They kissed and fondled and whispered words of
love. Neille's hips began to move, she could not
stop them, and when he thrust his thigh between
hers she abandoned herself to the pulsing rhythm
of love. He came into her.

'Oh!' Neille was whimpering again, filled with
incandescent delight.

He slid deep, then pulled back. She teetered on a
trembling edge—wanting, wanting, wanting.
Deeper he thrust. A pause. Another tremblingly
delicious edge. Then deeper still. Her head turned
wildly on the pillow. She gasped, clutching his
shoulders as her desire unleashed into desperate
need. Music pounded in her ears, filled her veins as
Jack thrust again and again, lifting her to a climax
as overwhelming and dramatic as a Sibelius
symphony.

CHAPRER TEN

JACK grinned over the top of his glass of champagne. 'I suppose now I'm expected to marry you?'

'Who says I'll have you?' she enquired, her blue eyes sparkling.

'Will you?'

Neille sipped, wrinkling her nose against the ping of the bubbles. 'I might, if you ask nicely.'

'Please, my darling Nellie, will you marry me?'

She put down her champagne, to cuddle close. 'Yes, my darling Jackson, I will.' Kisses replaced Moët et Chandon. 'After all, I've grown accustomed to your face.'

'How about growing accustomed to my body?' he enquired, with a mock leer. He nuzzled her bare shoulder. 'Say the word and I'll take you on a second guided tour. Sorry, third tour.'

'The word.'

Jack laughed. 'You're insatiable, which makes two of us. Yet maybe it would be wise to have a few minutes respite and recharge the batteries?'

She made big eyes. 'But you said——'

'Bug off,' he replied, rubbing the tip of his nose against hers. He settled back on the pillow, his arm around her. 'How about explaining what it was your father did which gives Lewis his hold? And don't you dare quote back at me that I said no questions earlier. I'm not perfect.'

'Yes, you are.' Neille threw him a sidelong

glance. 'No, you're not. Did you really have to nail me to the wall over Simon in such a brutal manner?'

The arm around her tightened. 'I could see no alternative. I expect you went home and cried, but——'

'I did, for two hours.'

'Forgive me?' he pleaded. 'But as I saw it, confronting the past in one fell swoop was by far preferable to being asked picky little questions over a drawn-out period, and I needed to know. Despite my accusations, I was aware you didn't give a damn about Lewis's money so I couldn't understand what tied you to him. I thought that if you told me about your relationship with Simon I'd find the key. I didn't. There didn't seem to be any common factor. Simon was like a rocket, shooting off into space, whereas Mr Mitchell comes over as an armoured tank.' Jack handed her her champagne glass and reached for his own. 'And your father's scared of being flattened?'

She nodded and took a sip of champagne. 'You remember I told you how my mother was ill for a full year before she died, and how all that time she'd been looked after by a private nurse? Well, those were the early days in Daddy's career when he didn't earn much, and private care is expensive. My mother should've gone into hospital, but apparently she had one of those irrational fears that if she was admitted she would never come out again, so she made Daddy promise she could stay at home. Because he doted on her and could never refuse her anything, he agreed.'

Jack kissed her shoulder. 'I can understand how he felt.'

'You're nice,' she smiled, then returned to her tale. 'My mother wasn't expected to survive for very long when the nurse was initially engaged so Daddy intended to finance the care from their savings; then she established herself on a plateau. Very quickly the savings ran out. Anything which could raise a few pounds, he sold, and all other expenses were trimmed to the bone, but it wasn't enough. Next Mooie and Uncle Ken contributed, and other members of the family, but as the months went by so that money disappeared. Daddy began to panic. He decided he would have to approach old Mr Mitchell for a loan. He'd worked in the accounts section for eight years, never once been late, never had time off sick, and had contributed hours and hours of unpaid overtime, but he met with an out-of-hand dismissal.' Neille sighed. 'Lewis's father regarded himself as a benevolent boss, but in reality he was as indifferent to his employees as his son. So my father didn't know where to turn.'

'Why didn't he borrow money from a bank?'

'I don't know. Obviously he wasn't thinking straight. He's not very good at keeping a cool head under pressure.'

'Difficult for anyone if their wife's dying at home,' Jack mused.

'Yes, but—well, my father was so aggrieved by Mr Mitchell's lack of compassion that he decided to borrow the money from the company secretly.'

'You mean he cooked the books?'

'Yes, but he was only *borrowing*,' she stressed. 'An insurance policy had been taken out to cover my mother's life, so two thousand pounds was due at her death. Daddy invented a make-believe firm which was supposed to supply Mitchells' with textiles, and paid money to them which he pocketed. In turn, he doled it out in wages to the nurse. He kept strict records, only took exactly what was needed, not a penny more, and set everything against the insurance policy.'

'But that was one hell of a risk!' Jack exclaimed.

'Not so much as you'd imagine, apparently. Mitchells' accounting system at the time was a cumbersome affair and whatever my father's other failings, he's smart with figures. According to him, inventing the false company and including it in the paperwork was easy.'

'So where did he go wrong?'

'By taking too much. You see, my mother clung on and on and the nursing costs soared way above the sum of the policy. After her death Daddy received the pay out and fed it back into Mitchells', but was still left with a hefty sum outstanding. He scrimped and saved, and over the next months paid back all he possibly could from his salary. He was within less than a hundred pounds of being in the clear when——' Neille let out a breath. 'Walter Rice spotted the textile firm.'

'And all hell was let loose?'

'With a vengeance! My father was marched off to see old Mr Mitchell, who ranted on about theft and embezzlement, which to be fair it was, and said he intended to inform the police. Daddy tried to explain how he'd been out of his mind with worry, and that all he owed now was less than a measly hundred, and at length Mr Mitchell agreed to reconsider. The matter was left in abeyance for a month.'

Jack winced. 'While your father sweated it out?'

'He said that month was sheer murder,' she agreed. 'He turned pale even telling me about it. However, the upshot was that Mr Mitchell agreed no action would be taken, in view of Daddy's promise to pay back the remaining amount within weeks.'

'But I don't see the connection with Lewis. All this happened twenty years ago when he'd have been a schoolboy. He wouldn't have been involved.'

'No, but Daddy *knows* Lewis knows about him taking the money. The ledgers which include entries of the textile firm remain stored in Mitchells' basement, and he's convinced Lewis is keeping them there on purpose.' She shifted uneasily on the pillow. 'Lewis resents criticism, and there've been episodes in the past involving his staff when he's been actively vindictive as a result of someone putting him down. That's where my dilemma springs from. If I cross him by ending our relationship myself, there's the possibility he might react by resurrecting Daddy's falsification of the accounts.'

'But a court case'd be impossible after all this time,' Jack protested.

'It wouldn't need to be that. Lewis could dismiss him and spread enough rumours to ensure he couldn't find another job.'

'I don't know why your father didn't leave Mitchells' long ago.'

Neille sighed. 'Because he doesn't like change, because he was afraid to disturb the status quo. Even now his attitude towards Lewis is two-edged. He's frightened of what he might do and yet he admires him for the successes he's made at Mitchells'. But even if Daddy was sacked, it's not so much finding another job which would matter so much as the strain he'd be placed under. His life would become a misery.'

'And to protect him from that, you chose to appear in saucy underwear.' It was a statement of fact. 'I suspected you of having qualms about playing the *risquée* lady all along.' Jack's brow furrowed. 'How high do you rate your chances of goading Lewis into giving you your walking papers?'

'They tend to fluctuate,' she confessed, feeling her heart plunge. 'But whenever I've dared reveal an extra bare inch in the past Lewis has done nothing but grumble.'

'The man must be mad,' he murmured, and lowered the sheet which had been tucked around her in order to plant a kiss between her breasts.

'The photographs should convince him I'm not suited to be a future Mrs Mitchell,' Neille insisted, a little breathlessly.

'I've been convinced of that for ages. The future Mrs Rea—yes. Mitchell?' Jack turned up his nose. 'Out of the question. And what's supposed to happen if this stunt of your falls flat? The next logical step would seem to be a centrefold in *Penthouse*, but you can scrap that, my darling. As from this minute nude poses are for my eyes only.'

'Yes, Jack,' Neille said obediently, her eyes dancing. Then her expression became grave. 'But my stunt won't fall flat. It mustn't!'

'Are you *sure* Lewis is aware of your father's . . . lapse?' he questioned. 'It seems a long shot that old man Mitchell would tell a schoolboy, and as the debt was insignificant isn't there a good chance of it having been forgotten by the time Lewis joined the business?'

'Ye-s, I suppose so.' She was doubtful. 'And no, I personally am not sure. Lewis has never hinted about the lapse to me. It's just that Daddy regards the fact he's not been made a member of the board as proof positive that he's regarded as suspect. Normally the chief accountant is offered a directorship as standard procedure,' she explained.

'But maybe he isn't a director because he's not a decisions man, or simply because he's too old?'

'It's possible,' Neille agreed, displaying little conviction. She changed course. 'What's been arranged about your company and Mitchells' security business?'

'I've given notice that we're pulling out. Pity, but—well. There'll be other chances. I'm meeting Lewis on Friday afternoon, just to square matters.'

'Friday afternoon? Perhaps by then he'll have declared me kaput?' she said hopefully.

'Perhaps. Apart from this gradual striptease, what else have you done to persuade him he's best rid of you? Picked your nose, drunk from the finger bowl, answered back?'.

'Not the first two, but I confess to trying with the third. But Lewis is so thick-skinned it's unbelievable. Also I've spent hours gabbling on about how serious relationships don't interest me, how——'

'No? Just wait until I have that wedding ring on your finger, my gorgeous Nellie; you'll change your tune.'

'Yes, Jack,' she murmured, as he kissed her. '*And* how I value my freedom,' she continued, when they surfaced. 'I even vowed my intention of cycling around the world, but it went straight over his head.'

'Maybe he thought you were playing hard to get?'

'It's possible.' Neille sighed. 'I've tried being flippant, I've tried being brusque, but nothing's penetrated. But, then, I've never dared go *too* far.'

'You haven't stamped on his ego with both feet, like you've stamped on mine?' He warded off a dig in the ribs. 'And Lewis still believes he's courting you?'

''Fraid so. But he'll change his mind on Friday when he opens his morning newspaper.' She gave Jack a look, suddenly stricken. 'If the gods are with me.'

Whether or not the gods were with her, the press did their bit. On Friday, when she saw the spread she had been granted, Neille was jubilant. For once she actually *liked* the media, for there were illustrated articles on three different women's pages and four quarter-page advertisements inserted by the fashion house. Open a newspaper, and there she was. Lewis just had to sit up, take notice, and topple backwards in horror.

Modelling assignments kept her busy from nine until mid-afternoon, and then she dashed home and waited. Surely he would ring? When the phone remained silent, she submitted to the strain. She prepared a cup of coffee and let it go cold. She dashed upstairs and forgot why. Tights were washed and left in the bowl. A second cup of coffee was percolated and neglected. Neille assembled a vast salad, then remembered her father was attending an accountants' soirée and would not be home until eleven. Well, Jack would be round. He'd promised to come round. He could eat the salad. She couldn't eat anything, not until Lewis called. And interspersed with all her rushing around were quick reassuring peeks at the newspapers. Yes, she did look sexy. Yes, that was a nipple shaded beneath white lace. Yes, the Montmartre shot did have an air of 'come up and see me sometime'. But the phone remained silent.

When the doorbell buzzed at six o'clock, she flew.

'Oh Jack, thank goodness you're here,' she babbled, covering him with grateful kisses. 'Do you want some salad? Lewis hasn't rung. Maybe he hasn't seen the papers? I mean, if he had he'd have rung already, wouldn't he? Or would he? Suppose he's seen them and he doesn't care?' Neille clung on to his arm as he steered her into the living room. 'You were with him this afternoon, did he say anything?'

'Nothing. After all it *was* a business meeting. And a stuffed shirt like Lewis is hardly going to discuss his personal likes and dislikes with someone he's only met once.'

'But what did he look like—disgruntled?'

Jack shook his head. 'Cool, calm and collected.'

She groaned. 'Couldn't you have slipped a mention of my photographs into the conversation?'

'I suppose I could, but I deliberately didn't. The impetus to drop you must come totally from Lewis himself. You wouldn't want him to suspect a put-up job?'

'No, but if he hasn't even seen the photographs and he still intends to propose——' Her voice began to waver. 'What do I do?'

'You say "no"—loud and clear. Because the photographs don't matter.'

'But——'

'No buts, just listen.' Jack dropped on to the sofa and pulled her down on to his knee. 'In winding up our business, Lewis and I discussed the mayhem that Walter Rice had created, and I said I felt your father had probably suffered more than anyone. It was not a chance observation, I'd said it in the hope of drawing Lewis out, and it worked. We talked on and he revealed two things.' Jack held up a finger. 'One, hard-working and devoted to his work as your father is, Lewis doesn't consider him suitable for the cut and thrust of the board, and two——' Another finger was raised. 'That in his opinion you father could be trusted with the Crown Jewels.'

Neille smiled delightedly. 'You are clever,' she said, hugging him.

'Einstein almost, but there's more. When I gave him my résumé of the past month, I explained that certain security aspects of his stores required attention. One was the risk of fire. I suggested we should go down to the basement where I'd point out prime examples. Earlier I'd been down there with my guards,' Jack explained, 'so I was able to march straight to a store, fling wide the door and denounce it as a tinder box. I wasn't that far wrong as it happens, though maybe I did do some acting. I told Lewis that one dropped cigarette end would have the files and ledgers which were crammed in there bursting into flame.'

'And what was his reaction?' she asked, when he broke off to grin.

'To declare the entire collection obsolete. He

checked the dates, discovered they covered a
period between eighteen and twenty-five years ago,
and said he'd no idea why such ancient ledgers
should have kept. Obviously it was an oversight.
At the clap of his hands a storeman came running,
and before we'd even left the basement the shelves
were half empty and a bonfire was blazing in an
incinerator.'

'Oh, Jack.' Weak with relief, Neille rested her
head on his shoulder. 'You've solved all my
problems—and Daddy's. There's only one word to
describe you.'

'Pachyderm?' he suggested.

'Wonderful.'

He grinned. 'Suppose we settle for wonderful
pachyderm?'

'Right.' She gave him several grateful kisses,
then smiled up. 'Shall we go to bed, my wonderful
pachyderm? The champagne is already on ice.'

Jack groaned. 'My God! Feminism strikes
again. Aren't I supposed to do the seducing?'

'You did it on Tuesday, Wednesday, Thursday,
so now it's my turn. And it's not feminism.' She
dug him in the ribs. 'It's a healthy sex drive,
zonko.'

'I believe you. And I'd love to go to bed, but
what about eating that salad?'

She gave him her wholesome *ingénue* smile.
'What salad? I don't know anything about a
salad.'

'I bet.' He tilted his head. 'Isn't that the phone?'

In the two seconds it needed to reach the
receiver, Neille's mood went topsy-turvy. From
being warm and happy, suddenly she was quaking.
In her head she knew Jack had eradicated Lewis

Mitchell as a threat, yet in her heart she was scared. The habit of a year was hard to break.

'H-hello?' she stammered.

'Lewis here,' her caller announced, in a brisker than usual staccato. 'Sorry, but this evening's impossible. A friend's flown in from Australia, a lady friend. Should have mentioned this Monday, but I forgot. Met Fiona while I was out there and teamed up. Instant attraction. Hope you don't mind, but plenty more fish in the sea. You're a pretty girl, you'll soon find someone else. Don't fret.'

'I won't,' she inserted, grinning at Jack, who had his ear pressed against the receiver.

'Join a club or two,' Lewis stampeded on. 'Take up golf.'

'Golf?' Jack mouthed soundlessly, rolling his eyes.

'I can give you an introduction to a decent course, but then again, perhaps you want to go cycling around the world? Well, I can't wait two years to raise a family. Need heirs. Owe it to Mitchells'. Business must come first. Chin up, Neille. Your turn will come. Prince Charming might just be around the corner.'

'Possible,' she agreed, digging Prince Charming in the ribs. Prince Charming groaned.

'Well, goodbye.' Lewis had reached the end of his appointed piece.

'Goodbye.'

Down went the phone.

'What a load of unadulterated——'

'Language, Jackson,' she cut in grinning. 'And don't we make a splendid pair? You take away his left arm crutch, *I* take away the right.'

'There's only one word to describe you.'

'Brilliant?' Neille suggested, unable to keep from smiling.

'Cruel. Not to Lewis, to me,' Jack said, when she gazed at him in surprise. 'Hell, your daily production of freelance insults, all geared to crush the unsuspecting male, was bad enough, but now you constantly inflict bodily pain. I must be a mass of bruises.' He heaved a loud and theatrical sigh, and walked to the stairs. 'I wouldn't be at all surprised if your next act is to flatten me.' He grinned and held out a hand. 'What do you think, my darling Nellie?'

She joined him, face flushed with love. 'I think, my wonderful pachyderm, there's a distinct possibility you could be right.'

ROMANCE

Variety is the spice of romance

Each month, Mills & Boon publish new romances. New stories about people falling in love. A world of variety in romance — from the best writers in the romantic world. Choose from these titles in July.

A WILLING SURRENDER Robyn Donald
PRISONER Vanessa James
ESCAPE FROM THE HAREM Mary Lyons
CAPTURE A SHADOW Leigh Michaels
GLASS SLIPPERS AND UNICORNS Carole Mortimer
THE WAITING MAN Jeneth Murrey
THE LONELY SEASON Susan Napier
BODYCHECK Elizabeth Oldfield
WIN OR LOSE Kay Thorpe
SHADOW PRINCESS Sophie Weston
*****SURRENDER, MY HEART** Lindsay Armstrong
*****WILD FOR TO HOLD** Annabel Murray

On sale where you buy paperbacks. If you require further information or have any difficulty obtaining them, write to: Mills & Boon Reader Service, PO Box 236, Thornton Road, Croydon, Surrey CR9 3RU, England.

*These two titles are available *only* from Mills & Boon Reader Service.

Mills & Boon
the rose of romance